BAMBOO
TERROR

BAMBOO
TERROR

*Treachery, terror and death
in the 1958 jungles of
North Viet Nam prior to the
intervention of U.S Forces*

William James Ross

To order additional copies of this book, contact:
Xlibris Corporation
1-888-795-4274
www.Xlibris.com
Orders@Xlibris.com
15483

CONTENTS

Also by William James Ross

The Ghost of Kamabara

The Adventures of Terry Tanuki, the Magical Raccoon

The Japanese translation of
Haragei for Kodansha

For Michie, who endured all those years

TOKYO—1958

In 1958, the war in Viet Nam was only a smoldering cinder—
the South against the North. The incidents that would start a
major war and change the history of the
Far East were just beginning to germinate.
This is the story of one group of people, who managed to change
a little bit of that history.

1.

MICHAEL HAZZARD, EXPATRIATE

TOKYO 1958

*T*his was the last time Michael Hazzard would walk down any street after dark with his mind a million miles away. Things only had to happen to him once, and he never made the same mistake twice.

He had gone about a hundred yards down the street after leaving his office, when suddenly he was grabbed from behind and slammed into the mouth of a small alley. Before he had a chance to come back out of his daydreaming, his arms were pinned behind him, and a rough scar-faced Oriental was using his belly and rib cage for a punching bag. Hazzard let fly with his right leg, and the toe of his shoe caught Scarface right where it hurt the most. While Scarface was doubling up like a wet noodle, Hazzard spun the one on his back around, grabbed his wrist, pushed, pulled, and snapped. The man let out a howl, and when he dropped to his knees, Hazzard gave him a face full of size 11 1/2 C.

There was a grunt behind him, and Hazzard turned to see

Scarface come lunging off the ground. Scarface must have either been stupid, or a rank amateur at this kind of rough and tumble business. One of the basic rules of fighting for keeps like this is; never stop to think after you grab your opponent. You have to react with an instantaneous conditioned reflex in everything you do—or you are dead.

Scarface's conditioned reflexes were probably limited to picking up beer glasses because he was now making one of the biggest mistakes of his life.

He threw himself forward, grabbed the front of Hazzard's shirt with both hands, and stopped. It took Hazzard so much by surprise he did not react too fast himself. But there he was, holding onto Hazzard's shirt front, and staring up with his mouth open in the classic expression of stupidity. Hazzard did not know what the hood was trying to prove, but he decided to give the quizzical look in the man's eyes a real fast answer. The oldest trick in the book.

He brought his arms up fast inside Scarface's bent elbows, then down behind his neck and pulled—all in one fast, smooth motion. At the same time Hazzard bent his head down. Scarface dropped his arms away from Hazzard's shirt as his nose smashed into the top of Hazzard's head. Hazzard had used this method so often he had become quite an expert at it. It is guaranteed to take the fight out of anybody. But if you try it, you've got to be very careful. It's like the old story of kissing a duck's ass without getting the feathers in your mouth. You've got to be fast!

Hazzard had just stepped back to take a good look at these two would-be roughhouse boys when somebody slipped silently up behind him with a blackjack.

All the tin cans and boxes in the alley seemed to start rushing up at Hazzard's face. Then, he suddenly realized they were not coming up. He was going down. He had not counted on there being a third one hidden in the alley, and he cursed himself for letting all the skills he had learned over the years go stale.

Just before Hazzard passed out he heard someone talking in

what he later would think was Chinese. Even though he could not understand the words, they sounded rough and commanding.

The sound of a noodle vendor's flute finally filtered into Hazzard's foggy brain and he slowly opened his eyes. For a moment he could not figure out where he was or what he was doing there. When he saw the tin cans and rubbish it all came back like a bad dream. He was soaked with sweat and stiff as a board. He grunted and groaned himself to a sitting position. It felt like a herd of elephants had been walking on his chest and stomach, and when he finally made it to his feet, he bent over and threw up all over the alley.

Nobody saw him as he staggered out onto the street. Even if someone had, it would not have bothered them very much. Japan is a weird country. Drunks were always staggering around and lying in the gutters. Even the police never bothered about them very much.

Hazzard was beat, and he knew it. There was a lump behind his ear throbbing like a jackhammer, and he found he could not take a deep breath if he straightened up.

He knew he had to find some place to lie down, and he had to find it fast. Everything was going round and round, and he could not focus his eyes on anything for more than a few seconds.

The nearest place was his office, and he fiddle-footed and stumbled along until he got back to the building. He thought he would never make the stairs. Every few steps he had to stop, kneel down, and grab the wall.

Inside the office he dragged a chair up to the little washbasin, sat and soaked his head under the running faucet. This only seemed to make the throbbing worse, and he thought he might drown in the basin if he passed out.

Gathering up a wet towel, he flopped his six-foot-two frame down on his five-foot-two Japanese couch and passed out as the room began to go around in circles.

Hazzard was in the middle of the Arctic Ocean, strapped to a big slab of ice, with the wind howling over his naked body. A short

distance away a group of beautiful nude Eskimo girls were danc-
ing around a big bonfire. They kept looking over at him, smiling
and winking. One big, tall, lanky one was keeping time by beating two little sticks together. Hazzard had to break loose and get
that tall one. He gave one big pull on the ropes, and bam!—he was
lying on the floor of his office.

He could hear the typewriter out in the small reception room;
that accounted for the two little sticks. Then, he looked up and
saw the fan; that accounted for the howling wind. Someone had
placed it at his feet, and when it blew over his sweat-heavy clothes,
it was just like an arctic blast. Bright sunlight was streaming through
the window, and the sight of it started his head throbbing again.
He switched off the fan, rolled back on the couch with a groan,
and put the towel over his face.

The typing stopped, and after a moment of silence, the towel
popped up. Hazzard opened one eye and gasped. Nothing could
hurt bad enough to make him close his eye again, and so, he opened
both eyes.

Michiko was bent over him peering down. It is hot in Tokyo
in August, and Hazzard had just discovered Michiko did not wear
a brassiere when it was hot in August. The low-necked blouse was
billowing out, the sunlight was streaming in, and there were two
of the cutest little breasts Hazzard had ever seen.

She had been working for Hazzard ever since he had started
out in his unsuccessful business six months before, and he had
never thought she could be built like this. Most Japanese girls
aren't. Maybe it had been the baggy skirts and blouses she had
always worn before, he was thinking. Hazzard shook his head slowly
and decided it was time to take a new look at his Girl Friday.

Michiko had been in the office for six months, and he just
now realized he had never really noticed her before. I must be
slipping, he thought.

"Mike-san, *daijobu desuka?*" she asked.

He snapped out of his dreaming and looked up at her face.
She had lovely dark almond-shaped eyes. The kind women are

always faking with eyebrow pencils, only Michiko's were real. Hazzard found himself wondering what other hidden mysteries of the Orient she came equipped with.

"Mike-san, you all right?" she asked again.

"Yeah, I'm all right," he said and tried to lift himself up to a sitting position. "I've just got the world's biggest headache, that's all." This little bit of effort made the bells in his head sound off again, and he flopped back down on the couch with a grunt.

Michiko straightened up, put her hands on her hips, and with a 'mother-scolding-the-little-boy' look in her eyes, she said, "Hangover, ne? You should be more careful. Not drink so much."

"I wish it was a hangover," he said, and reached back to caress the grapefruit-size knot behind his ear. Then, he looked up at Michiko. "What are you doing here so early in the morning, my little flower of the Orient?" he groaned as he managed to slowly sit up again.

This caused a big widening of those lovely dark eyes and a burst of Japanese girly giggles. "Early morning? It is almost time for lunch," she quipped. "Mike-san, what did you drink last night?"

She cocked her head and looked at him sideways through half closed lids. This made the skin on Hazzard's back start goose-stepping down his spine. He had an almost uncontrollable urge to grab her and take a nip out of one of those exquisitely shaped ears. He had long ago discovered it set off a remarkable chain reaction in most women. He found himself wondering if Michiko knew about this. He shook his head. The blow behind the ear must have really jarred his brain out of place. This train of thought was not going to get him anywhere except into trouble, and he forced himself to look at the floor. It needed sweeping, and so did the inside of his head.

"Michiko, do we have any aspirin?" he asked.

"Yes. How many do you want?"

"A whole bottle. The large economy size."

Michiko sighed and went out to her desk in the small reception room. Hazzard watched her go and shook his head again. As much as he knew about the Orient, he would never be able to figure out the women. He had not paid Michiko for the last two months, and in spite of his continuous bad humor and ordering her around like a servant, she seemed to have no complaints and kept coming to the office every morning. She treated him like a little child most of the time. Making him carry an umbrella at the slightest hint of rain; forcing cold tablets on him if he so much as sneezed; lecturing him to eat more vegetables; change his shirt at the least sign of dirt; and cut down on his intake of beer and whiskey. Just like a mother . . . or a wife!

The thought of all this made Hazzard suddenly sit up straight on the couch. These things had been happening for the last six months, and the warning bells were just now going off. The last thing he wanted right now was to be tied down by marriage. He had more things to think about, and getting emotionally involved with Michiko would only complicate everything.

Ever since the Korean War, Hazzard's life had been one big jumble of mixed-up events. He had been captured by the Chinese, released after the war, almost given a general court-martial, spent a year in an army hospital with tuberculosis, disability retired from the army, and then decided to return to Japan to study the language.

*   *   *

He had run into an old friend, Lieutenant Bill Madden, at Tenth Corps Headquarters in Korea and accepted an invitation to visit Madden at his outfit's command post, the 555th Artillery Battalion, commonly called The Triple Nickels. A week later he had telephoned Madden and driven a jeep up to the battalion CP to drink over old times. That night the Chinese broke through the South Korean division up north, and before they had a chance to realize what was happening, the Reds were swarming all over them.

The rest of the war was spent in various prison camps in North Korea. The communists never did find out Hazzard was an intelligence officer, and had assumed he was just another artillery captain. The war ended and Hazzard was sent back through Panmunjom where the prisoner of war exchange was taking place. From there he was sent to St. Luke's Army Hospital in Tokyo.

Three days later he received two of the biggest shocks of his life, one after the other. The first one came when the doctor had informed him he had tuberculosis. The second shock came in the afternoon when a major from the Adjutant General's office visited him. As an intelligence officer in possession of certain knowledge vital to the security of the United States, he had placed himself in a position where he had fallen into the hands of the enemy. This was something every intelligence officer is constantly warned about.

The government was now preparing charges against Captain Michael Hazzard, which, if investigation showed he had collaborated with the enemy in any form whatsoever, would lead to a general court-martial.

Everything had finally come out all right, but not until after he had sweat out six months at Fitzsimons Army Hospital in Denver, Colorado. The government had dropped all charges, and the ward doctor had told him all traces of tuberculosis had cleared up completely under medication. There would be no operation necessary. Another six months of hospitalization ended with Hazzard being retired from service with a monthly pension.

He took an apartment in Denver, bought a second-hand car, and spent a hell-bending three months tomcatting through the Rocky Mountains. The day finally came when all the money he had saved during his year in the hospital was only a memory. It was time to think about doing something serious.

Learning he had four years of schooling coming to him under the GI Bill of Rights, he decided to return to Japan and study Japanese. With a working knowledge of the language under his belt, he would apply for a position with the State Department and hopefully be assigned to the embassy in Tokyo.

He had thrown himself into studying the language with a

passion, and spent his evenings practicing karate in a small dojo in his neighborhood.

Within two years he had given up the idea of ever working for the State Department. He had met too many of the hundreds of Americans working in the Tokyo embassy, and the stories they told about efficiency reports, personality conflicts, petty jealousies, drinking problems, etc. had turned him off. It sounded like the army all over again.

He also felt he would never be fluent in the language, and knew he would never become an expert in karate. Though he had these reservations about himself, he still knew he could handle enough of the language to get along with almost everyone he met— and he could handle himself better than any street thug he would run up against.

Four years had gone swiftly by, and suddenly the monthly checks for his studies under the GI Bill of Rights stopped coming. The honeymoon was over.

It was then he conceived the idea of opening a private detective agency in Tokyo. He would be the only foreigner in the business, and his knowledge of both the language and karate would insure him of a steady clientele. It had been a pregnant idea, but the result was stillborn.

Hazzard still longed for the excitement and thrill of the dangers and brain-taxing challenge his life as an intelligence officer had offered, but a foreign private detective in Japan was something that astounded the Japanese government officials. The main reason seemed to be because it had never been done before, and to the Oriental mind this was enough to keep Hazzard from getting a license.

It had taken six months, tons of paper work, miles of red tape, and countless interviews with polite but obstinate officials before he was allowed to go into business.

He had so many restrictions on what he could and could not do it hardly seemed worth while, but after going through all the red tape and constant frustrations, he had decided to stick it out.

With his license had come a warning, very polite, but a warning. One mistake, and he was out of business.

He thought over the last few months he had been in business. The complete absence of clients, and the steadily mounting pile of bills sitting unpaid on his desk. It was beginning to look like he would never have a chance to make a mistake before Private Eye Michael Hazzard folded up.

His apartment, office rent, and food took most of his pension, leaving him only a few thousand yen every month to buy an occasional beer. Everything else was on a 'catch-me-if-you-can' payment basis. When the mail came it was always from people asking for payments on something or other. When the phone rang it was the same people. They were sorry to bother him, but when was he going to pay? He hated to owe money to anyone, but he was now being slowly squeezed by the vise of bankruptcy and he could think of no possible way to pay off his creditors.

If something did not come up within the next few months, he knew he would have to leave the country and return to the United States. He would never be able to renew his visa in Japan with a bankruptcy behind him. He could only wait, hope, and worry. In this business you did not go out and grab customers in off the street. You could only advertise and sit waiting for the phone to ring or the door to open. If there was a list of first-class jerks in the world somewhere, Hazzard figured his name was probably on top.

The sound of raised voices from outside the door cut into his thoughts. Someone was talking in rapid, angry Japanese. A man's voice in high pitched falsetto. Michiko was *sumimasen*-ing him to death. The aspirins were late, the racket was pressing on his already splitting skull, and Hazzard did not like the tone of man's voice. He was just about to go out and tell the man to take a flying leap at the moon when he heard the outer door slam, and Michiko appeared as unruffled as ever, with the box of aspirin in her hand.

"Here, aspirin," and she handed the box to Hazzard as she continued on to the sink for a glass of water.

"Who were you talking to out there?" he asked.

"Oh, I do not know. Just some man asking for money."

"Another bill collector," mumbled Hazzard. He looked up at her almond eyes and she smiled gayly back. "Michiko, why do you keep working for such a stupid boss?"

This was a question she dared not answer truthfully, and all she could manage was a widening of her eyes and a small, "Eh?"

Hazzard opened the box of aspirin. There were only three little white pills left. He took the glass of water from Michiko and swallowed them all.

"You know, Michiko," he said, going into a reflective mood. "Tokyo needs an American private detective like I need another hole in the head. In business for six months and the only client we've had was a little old German lady who wanted me to find her lost poodle." He got up and walked to the window. The knot on the back of his head started to throb again. He could see down the street to where he had met Scarface and company the night before. Then, half to himself, he muttered, "And last night I get worked over in the alley. Why?"

Michiko's puzzled voice came from behind him. "Worked over?"

Hazzard was forever explaining the meaning of odd English phrases to Michiko and other people he ran into in his wanderings around Tokyo, but this time he decided it would be better to evade the question.

"Oh, never mind. You wouldn't understand." He saw the pouting look of disappointment on Michiko's face, and quickly added, "Well, Lotus Blossom, I think I still have enough loose change to take both of us to lunch. It probably will be the last meal either of us will ever eat, so we might as well make the most of it."

The expression on Michiko's face changed to smiles and girlish glee. Hazzard reached out and brushed back a curl that had fallen over Michiko's forehead. She seemed to like this and leaned forward. Then, the telephone rang. Hazzard cursed to himself. He did not know whether Alexander Graham Bell had intended it or not, but his gadget seemed to have an uncanny way of screwing things up in royal fashion.

"It's for you," Michiko said as she handed him the phone.

Putting his hand over the mouthpiece, Hazzard whispered, "Who is it?"

This brought on the famous Oriental answer, a wide-eyed, smiling shrug.

"Hello," said Hazzard in his best detective voice.

"Is this Mr. Hazzard?" said a man's voice.

"Yes . . ."

The voice was right out of the movies. If the man now said his name was Sidney Greenstreet and he wanted a detective to help him find a Maltese Falcon, Hazzard would believe him.

"My name is Brown. John Brown," said the voice.

Hazzard thought the man could have at least picked a more original name to go with the voice.

"Mr. Hazzard," the voice continued. "I have a small matter of urgent business I would like to discuss with you at your earliest convenience. Preferably today."

"That would be fine, Mr. Brown. Just one moment please." Hazzard held his hand over the mouthpiece again and winked at Michiko. The pause was supposed to impress Brown that Hazzard was a busy man and had to consult his schedule.

"If you could come over about . . ."

"I shall be at your office this afternoon at exactly one thirty," interrupted Brown.

Hazzard stared at the phone for a moment and then mumbled, "Why, yes, that would be fine . . ."

"Thank you very much, Mr. Hazzard. Good-bye," and John Brown hung up.

Hazzard slowly put the phone down. It could be a gag, he thought. The voice and then the name. No, it was too ridiculous not to be true. He looked at Michiko. "Let's go eat," he said, and they went out for a bowl of noodles. Things might be looking up. John Brown might be just what was needed to pay the rent.

*   *   *

John Brown, a heavy set, cultured, Sidney Greenstreet type of man, sat back comfortably in his leather chair behind the large, highly polished, mahogany desk in his study after carefully replacing the telephone receiver in its cradle. He made a tent with his fingers, and looked intently at the three men sitting opposite him across the desk.

The two thugs had not fared too well the night before. One of them had his arm and shoulder heavily bandaged and strapped in a tight sling. The one with the scar on his face could barely see over the large bandage covering his crushed nose.

Mr. Brown let his gaze wander over the two burly thugs. Then, he glanced at the third man and spoke in a calm even voice. "Well, Chang, he is still alive."

"I told you we did not kill him," the man replied in well educated English, his dark eyes flashing as he sensed the slight sarcasm in Brown's voice. "He might have a large bump on his head, but other than that, he does not have a scratch."

Brown nodded his head toward the two thugs. "Well, these two idiots do not look very healthy today. Looking at them, I find it hard to believe our Mr. Hazzard does not even have a scratch."

"Our Mr. Hazzard," replied the exasperated Chang. "Happens to have been trained in karate. I wish you had told us that little fact before we met him last night. Then these two wouldn't have come out so badly."

"Perhaps."

"Perhaps you did not know," said Chang with a touch of sarcasm.

Mr. Brown smiled. "Oh, I knew. There is very little I do not know about him. But telling you would have spoiled the fun. Besides, I am sure you wanted to know if the man was a coward or not. Isn't that what you told me? You were afraid his time in a prisoner of war camp might have changed his character, but looking at these two, I see it hasn't. You admit you are satisfied with the results?"

Chang nodded his head in agreement. "Yes, I am satisfied. But we have no time to waste."

"I am very anxious to meet Mr. Hazzard in person myself. It seems he is just the man we have been looking for," Brown stopped to look at his watch. "I am meeting him at one thirty. Leave the rest to me."

Chang grunted a reply and rose quickly from his chair. The two thugs followed meekly as he walked to the door.

Brown waited until he heard them leave the house. Then, he opened the top drawer of his desk with a small silver key that hung from his watch chain, and carefully withdrew a small, unpainted wooden box. Reaching into the drawer again, he took out several plain large, fat brown manila envelopes and placed them and the wooden box in his leather briefcase. From a side drawer he picked up a small automatic pistol, checked to make sure it was loaded, and slipped it into his pocket.

A glance at his watch told him it was now time to leave for the office of Michael Hazzard, private investigator.

John Brown smiled to himself as he settled his bulky form in the soft leather rear seat of his chauffeured Mercedes-Benz. Yes, it was going to be very interesting to meet the man called Michael Hazzard upon whom so much time and money had been spent. It was to be hoped that Mr. Hazzard was worth all the trouble.

*   *   *

2.

A STRING OF BEADS

It was now two o'clock. Mr. Brown had been as punctual as a new thousand dollar Rolex watch. At exactly one thirty he had walked through the door and introduced himself to Michiko. For the next thirty minutes Brown had steered the conversation into Hazzard's past activities by expert questioning. Hazzard was alert to this, but conversed freely with the stout man, parrying those questions that skipped over delicate subjects as expertly as the questioner.

Hazzard was amazed at the physical resemblance Brown had to the actor, Sidney Greenstreet. The cultured speech, the mannerisms, even the bulk. But now the novelty was wearing thin. John Brown had sat calmly listening and asking questions with his briefcase and hat held firmly on his lap. It was another hot day, and Hazzard was beginning to show visible signs of impatience. Mr. Brown had just noticed a picture on the wall of Hazzard in karate practice clothes, and was starting off on another tangent.

"Ah, that picture, Mr. Hazzard. You studied judo?"

"No," came the weary reply. "Karate. But Mr. Brown, as much

as I appreciate your interest, you have yet to tell me why you came to see me."

"Ah, yes," said the Greenstreet voice, in what sounded like a rasping sigh. "Mr. Hazzard, it is but a simple task." He took the small, unpainted wooden box from his briefcase, and placed it on the desk in front of Hazzard. "I would like you to deliver this small article for me."

"Who do I deliver it to?"

"To a friend of mine in Saigon," came the Greenstreet reply.

"Saigon?"

"Yes," and as calmly as if he were buying a new hat, Mr. Brown explained. "I am prepared to pay you the sum of ten thousand dollars for the safe delivery of the contents of this little box. Five thousand now, and the balance upon your return."

The impact of this statement had caught Hazzard by surprise. Only a weak sound came from his throat as he repeated the words, "Ten thousand dollars!" He made a quick mental calculation. "That's three million six hundred thousand yen!"

Hazzard looked at the box on the desk for a long time. Then, reaching over slowly, he picked it up and glanced over at Mr. Brown. Sidney Greenstreet-Brown sat unmoving, a knowing smile on his face. Hazzard decided there was no opposition to his opening the box, and he lifted the cover. He did not know what he had expected to find, but the sight of a small string of beads was somewhat disappointing.

Hazzard looked up and asked, "What is it?"

"It is a string of Buddhist prayer beads," replied Greenstreet-Brown in his most mysterious manner.

Again Hazzard looked into the box. "How much is this thing worth?"

Greenstreet-Brown gazed upwards at the ceiling, puckered up his lips in thought for a moment, and then replied. "Oh, I should say about four or five dollars."

"Four or five dollars!" Hazzard could not hide the amazement in his voice. "And you're willing to pay me ten thousand dollars just to deliver it to someone in Saigon?" His voice came back to normal and he smiled as he placed the box back on the desk. "Mr. Green . . . er, Brown, something smells awful fishy." He leaned over in a confidential manner and lowered his voice. "What's the angle? Dope? Jewels? Secret documents?"

This did not seem to bother the cultured manners of Greenstreet-Brown in the least. "There is no, what was the word? Ah, yes, angle. Let us say I represent a very rich, and somewhat eccentric client, who does strange things and pays excellent wages for services rendered. I assure you, Mr. Hazzard, there is nothing illegal, immoral, or as you put it, fishy about this in the least."

Hazzard looked across the desk, straight into the eyes of Brown. There had to be something else, things just did not happen this way. "Just take these beads to Saigon. Nothing else?"

Greenstreet-Brown returned the steady gaze. "Nothing else," he said smoothly.

Hazzard sat back in his chair, put his hand up to rub his chin, and studied the well-dressed Mr. John Brown. Here was a man offering an almost unbelievable proposition. The way he looked Hazzard in the eye when he spoke made him either a very honest man, or a lunatic. Hazzard stopped to dwell upon the possibility of Brown begin a little deranged.

"I can't figure out who yet, but one of us has got to be crazy," he said.

Mr. Brown smiled, and Hazzard could see Greenstreet-Brown was comfortable in knowing he was not the one who was crazy.

"Who do I deliver the beads to?" asked Hazzard. "If I accept the job."

"Sorry, Mr. Hazzard, but you will discover that only if, and when, you agree to deliver the beads."

John Brown was also thinking. Hazzard was a suspicious, but honest man. Talk alone would not convince him to deliver the beads, but Brown knew other things. He knew about the unpaid rent, the many bills, the lack of clients.

He opened his briefcase again, took out the large fat brown

manila envelopes and laid them on the desk. Then, in a calm, matter-of-fact voice, he spoke.

"Here are three envelopes. One contains five thousand American dollars. The other two contain a like sum in Japanese yen. As a retainer, you may have your choice of either currency."

Hazzard picked up the envelopes, one after the other, and examined their contents. The money was there, just as Mr. Brown had said it was. Five packs of American ten dollar bills and eighteen packs of one thousand yen notes. He didn't bother to count the money, realizing it would be just a waste of time. Then, he reached out, took the beads in one hand, and holding two of the envelopes in the other, he mentally weighed them against each other.

He could still smell a rat somewhere in the deal, but he could not put his finger on just what it was that kept trying to warn him. After the workout in the alley, maybe he was just being over-cautious.

"All right, Mr. John Brown, or whoever you are, I'll play your silly game. But I'm warning you, no tricks. This deal still has a fishy smell, in fact a great big fishy smell. Nobody goes around offering this much money just to deliver little strings of five dollar beads unless there is something more to it than meets the eye. I'm going to play along until I find out what that something is—then, maybe, I'll stop and come back here looking for you."

"Fine. I certainly hope you will come back here looking for me," smiled Brown.

Hazzard thought Brown had agreed a little too fast, but now he was committed. "Okay. I'll take the yen, if you don't mind. Now, who do I deliver the beads to?"

Mr. Brown took the envelope containing the dollars and placed it back in his briefcase. "The person's name is Ling Ling Yung."

"Ling Ling Yung?" and Hazzard smiled. "The name is almost as weird as this whole crazy idea."

Brown appeared not to have heard this last remark as he brought out another envelope from his briefcase. "Here are your tickets and travel instructions, Mr. Hazzard, with an additional five hundred dollars for any odd expenses you might have. You will follow these instructions to the letter, without any deviations."

"This is getting more like the army every minute," quipped Hazzard as he took the envelope. "Getting real pushy with the orders."

"Need I remind you, Mr. Hazzard?" said the cold Greenstreet voice. "I have just purchased ten thousand dollars worth of rights to give you orders."

There was a dramatic pause while Brown allowed this to sink in. Hazzard met the stern looking eyes with a sheepish grin. Okay, he'd play it any way Brown wanted. At least until he discovered the angle. Then we would see what we would see.

Brown went on speaking. "You will fly to Taipei the day after tomorrow. From there you will take the train to Chilung on the northern part of the island, where you will board a coastal steamer. The Queen Wilhelmina III, I believe it is called. It will take you to Saigon by way of Hong Kong. Detailed instructions are in the envelope, including letters to the embassies of Taiwan and South Viet Nam for you to obtain the proper visas for travel in their countries."

"Oh? . . . Hold on a minute," interrupted Hazzard. "It'll take a week or more to get visas for those countries . . ."

"I am perfectly aware of the bureaucratic delays in obtaining visas. So, I took the liberty of applying for your visas a month ago. They are ready and waiting. All you have to do is take your passport with those letters."

Hazzard sat back in amazement. "You certainly were sure of yourself, weren't you? What if I had said no?"

"But you didn't, did you?"

Hazzard couldn't help but laugh as he started to examine the contents of the envelope to see if there were any more surprises waiting for him.

Finally he looked up. "There's no return ticket."

"That will be furnished to you at the other end of your journey—when and if you deliver the beads."

Everything seemed rather reasonable except the word 'if'. Well, that would be something to think about in Saigon.

"Okay, Mr. Brown, you've got yourself a deal. But there's just one more little thing."

"Yes?"

"How do I find this Ting-a-ling-yung character?"

The look in Brown's eyes said the jest at the name was not funny. "Just arrive in Saigon. It will not be necessary for you to find anyone. You will be contacted. The person who says to you; There is terror in the bamboo only for the wicked, will be Ling Ling Yung."

Hazzard repeated the strange phrase. "There is terror in the bamboo only for the wicked . . ."

"It is from an almost forgotten Oriental proverb inscribed on the wall of an ancient temple in the jungles of Indo-China," explained Brown. "The complete proverb reads; There is terror in the bamboo only for the wicked, the good shall find only peace."

More mystery. It was beginning to take on the flavor of a Fu Man Chu novel. But to Hazzard, ten thousand dollars was still ten thousand dollars, and as far as he was concerned, he had just become the highest paid delivery boy in the Orient.

"And how do I get in touch with you, Mr. Brown?"

The briefcase snapped shut, and Greenstreet-Brown was rising ponderously to his feet. "It will not be necessary to get in touch with me. You have all the information necessary to complete this small task."

"I mean, when I come back. A little matter of a five thousand dollar balance."

Brown looked down at Hazzard and smiled his best Greenstreet smile. "Do not worry, Mr. Hazzard," he said in his best Greenstreet voice. "I shall contact you immediately, if and when you return."

There it was again, the 'if'.

Brown turned and strode magnificently toward the door. Hazzard sat spellbound. It was just like the movies. For a moment

Hazzard thought Brown was going to leave without another word, but he paused with his hand on the doorknob and turned around.

"Mr. Hazzard, do you own a gun?"

"No, I don't," Hazzard lied. "It's against the law here in Japan for anyone except the police and the military to have handguns."

Brown gave him a knowing smile. "Yes, of course."

"Why do you ask?"

"Just a passing thought. They are marvelous devices for self protection in experienced and skilled hands. Oh, yes, one more thing. The wooden box the beads came in. You may take it apart and examine it if you wish. It is not even necessary to take the box with you. Just deliver the beads. Above all, no matter what happens to you, you must keep the beads upon your person at all times." He paused to smile. "Farewell, Mr. Hazzard, and have a pleasant trip," and with that, he was gone, shutting the door behind him before Hazzard could say a word.

Hazzard sat for a few minutes looking at the door through which Mr. Brown had passed, beginning to wonder what he had gotten himself involved in. Perhaps Brown had a hypnotic effect on people. Then, he let his gaze fall on the small wooden box. He smiled as he thought how Mr. Brown had read his mind. It was obvious he would think something was hidden inside. Picking it up, he examined it, and slowly applied pressure until it snapped at the sides. It was just an ordinary wooden box, and he threw the pieces into the wastebasket. Next, the beads. Nothing unusual there either. Each bead was transparent enough to eliminate the possibility of anything being secreted in them.

Hazzard swiveled his chair around to face the window and began to think. Everything was too simple, too mysterious, and the price was too high. Something was definitely wrong. There was only one way to find out what it was—go along with the instructions until he came across it.

He began to think over everything Brown had said. Twice there had been an 'if'. Then, there were two other things that didn't set too well. Why had Brown mentioned a gun was a marvelous device for self protection in experienced hands? Maybe Brown knew a little too much about Michael Hazzard. And Brown's parting shot about keeping the beads on him at all times . . ."no matter what happens to you . . ."

The more Hazzard thought about it, the more it began to smell like stale herring. Delivering the beads might not be as simple as it seemed.

Then, with a grunt, he rose and went to the small clothes closet in the corner of the room. Pushing aside his raincoat, a broom, and a few boxes revealed a small hole in the baseboard. Sticking a finger in the hole, he pulled, and the baseboard came away from the wall. A portion of the wall behind the baseboard had been cut away, leaving a hole about eight inches wide and four inches high. Reaching inside, Hazzard pulled out a small package wrapped in dusty newspaper.

The baseboard, the boxes, and the other things were replaced, and Hazzard surveyed them for a moment to make sure Michiko would not become suspicious and discover the hiding place.

Going to the door he quietly turned the lock on the handle. Then he returned to his desk and unwrapped the newspaper. Underneath was a layer of oilcloth that he carefully unfolded. Inside was a well-oiled, short-barreled Colt MK III .357 magnum revolver and a box of cartridges.

Hazzard smiled affectionately as he took a cloth from a desk drawer and wiped away the excess oil. Then, holding the revolver cradled in his hand, he said, "Hello Sam, long time no see. You've had a long rest, and now you and me are going on a little trip."

He placed the beads in a money belt around his waist. As an afterthought, he put five packs of thousand yen notes inside the money belt with the beads and stuck another pack in his pocket. Sam was loaded and stuck inside his shirt under the money belt. He put the remaining cartridges in a small leather pouch and dropped it in his pocket. Looking in the mirror over the sink, he decided he needed a shave, and maybe a new shirt. He scooped up the remaining money and walked out to stand in front of Michiko's little desk.

"I'm going out to the barber shop. Call the Mikado and reserve a table for two next to the stage for the second show tonight," he told her, trying to look nonchalant.

Michiko's heart almost stopped. "You are going out tonight?"

"Yes, and don't look so sad. Here!" and he dropped 12 packs of thousand yen notes, one at a time, all over the top of her desk. "Go get your hair fixed, and change your clothes, or whatever you girls do when you go to the Mikado. Meet me in the lobby of the New Japan Hotel at seven o'clock. Tonight we dine, and tomorrow we start paying off a few bills. Okay?"

Michiko's eyes went from Hazzard to the money and back again. "Oh, Mike-san . . ."

But Mike-san was already going down the stairs, grinning from ear to ear. He bounced briskly out the door and nodded to all the people who stopped to stare. "Oh, I know what you're thinking," he said to himself. "There goes another one of those crazy foreigners. And this time they're right!"

A barber shop is a good place to think, that is if the barber shop is in Japan and you happen to be a foreigner. The barber figures he can't talk to you because of the language barrier, and he doesn't try. In America it would be the last place in the world where anyone would go to do his thinking. American barbers are all either baseball experts or frustrated politicians. Once they have you strapped in the tonsorial seat, they talk your ears off.

Right now Hazzard was thinking, and for once he wished he was in an American barber chair. At least the talk would keep his mind from wondering about John Brown and the little string of beads.

He realized the deal had gone off too quickly. It seemed like a thousand questions were running around unanswered in his still slightly aching head. Why was Brown willing to pay so much money to have an almost worthless string of beads delivered to someone in Saigon? Items that cheap could be sent by registered mail with no trouble. It meant there had to be something else to make them important enough to be carried and delivered by hand.

He had been too quick to grab the money. Hazzard was mentally kicking himself for being stupid, until he remembered this was the kind of weird business a private investigator got himself into, and nobody had twisted his arm.

After the barber shop, Hazzard went home to his small two room apartment in Shibuya. The business of the beads, and the ambush in the alley were now making him overcautious. He kept checking to make sure he was not being followed. When he arrived at his apartment, he eased himself through the door and systematically inspected each room, all the while keeping his hand inside his shirt ready to introduce Sam to any uninvited guest. He felt a little foolish when everything turned out as normal as it should be.

He took a shower and changed his clothes. Tonight was going to be the first time he had taken Michiko any place except for an occasional lunch. He remembered the way she had looked at him in the office when he had told her about the Mikado, and began to wonder if he was really doing the right thing. Mixing business with pleasure never had been a good idea, and a girl like Michiko might be a little more than he could handle once he got her out of the drab surroundings of the office and into the plush atmosphere of a night club.

It had taken longer than he had expected to catch a taxi, and it was almost seven thirty when Hazzard arrived at the New Japan Hotel. He strode through the automatic doors half expecting to find a missing Michiko, but there she was, sitting wide-eyed and pretty on one of the lobby sofas.

She saw Hazzard coming across the lobby and a fleeting expression of relief flashed across her lovely face. Then, she smiled and stood. Hazzard almost tripped on one of the idiotic high-tufted rugs the hotel had spread around the middle of the lobby. Michiko was a rather something in her office uniform of sweater, blouse, and skirt—but in a cocktail dress, she was fabulous.

This had been Hazzard's office girl for six months, and he never even knew it. Her hair was swept back along the sides and up in the back. A white feather tiara was fixed along one side and curved upwards over her jet-black hair. The gold brocade cocktail dress was low cut and clung to every curve of her body like another layer of skin. High-heeled gold pumps accentuated the calf muscles to show a perfect set of legs.

Hazzard gulped, and found his voice as he came up to where she stood, and almost lost it again when he got a whiff of the perfume she was wearing.

"I'm sorry to be late," he mumbled.

"It's all right," she said.

Hazzard said nothing, and there was a long embarrassing pause.

"Well, ah, shall we go?" he asked.

"Yes," she said.

There was another pause as Hazzard just stood and stared at her. Then, he caught himself and smiled.

"Shall we go?"

Michiko giggled. "That is the second time you say the same thing."

Hazzard shook his head. So it was. He reached out, took her arm, and guided her outside. As they crossed the lobby, Hazzard was conscious of the gawking tourists. The scowling looks on the female faces and the lecherous leers on the male faces. The two and three-week wonders going around the world before it was too late. Plane loads of doddering old busybodies passing judgement on all foreign men with Oriental girls. As they passed through the automatic doors he stuck his tongue out at one shocked lady who was leering at them through a pince-nez.

A little revenge for past insults, he thought.

Over dinner at the Mikado they watched the floor show that was always tops at this palace-like theater restaurant, and talked of many things—mostly about Michiko. Hazzard hadn't realized how little he actually knew about his office girl. From now on, he promised himself, he would spend more time thinking about personnel problems and less about unpaid bills.

Michiko had graduated from Doshisha University in Kyoto. Her father was chairman of the board of a large Kyoto bank. Her sister was an airline stewardess and her brother was still in college. She had led a rather strict life at home with her father keeping a tight rein on all her activities. She had to be home every night before ten. She could not go out with anyone unless her father approved beforehand, and at night she had to give a detailed account of everything she had done and where she had gone during the day.

One day, she managed to get enough courage to tell her father she was going to Tokyo to find a job and support herself. To her surprise, he had agreed and only warned her about the type of work she chose. It would have to be dignified and not anything to bring disgrace on the family name. She had been in Tokyo three days when she had seen Hazzard's small classified ad in The Japan Times.

Watching her talk was fascinating. So much so, Hazzard never remembered seeing the fabulous show at the Mikado. Before he realized it, he was asking her if she would like to see his apartment. Her answer almost floored him.

"Yes," she said. "I would like to very much. I have wanted to see where you live for a long time."

All the way across town in the taxi to Shibuya Hazzard held her hand. Every time he squeezed, she squeezed back.

When they arrived, Hazzard began to worry if he had left the apartment in its usual mess. As the door opened and the light went on, he heaved a sigh of relief. He thought it looked quite presentable. Then, he saw Michiko's face. She was frowning and shaking her head.

"Yappari!" she said. "You can tell a man lives here."

Hazzard shrugged his shoulders. Well, he thought, you can't win them all, and followed her meekly around the apartment. She was interested in everything. She puttered around the small kitchen that occupied the wall of one room, stuck her head in the Japanese-style bathroom, glanced at all the books, ran her finger along the window sills, wanted to know if he had a maid, and who did the cooking.

When she learned there was no maid, and he did the cooking, she smiled. "It is very nice," she said as she turned around from inspecting the bedroom.

"Very nice," repeated Hazzard, only he was looking at Michiko. Suddenly, the perfume of her hair became intermixed with the Scotch and waters he had had at the Mikado, and he reached out for her. She was in his arms and they were kissing. Hazzard could feel the fast beat of her little heart as he crushed her to him. Then, still holding her tight, he snuggled his face into the side of her neck and took the lobe of her delicately shaped ear between his teeth. Michiko stiffened and rose up on her toes against him.

"Michiko," he whispered. "Will you stay here tonight with me?"

"I don't know," she answered, and pushing herself away, she walked past him to the living room.

Hazzard could not understand this piece of Oriental female logic. Either you do or you don't, he thought, but Hazzard still had much to learn of a woman's heart. Especially if the woman was Japanese.

"Why don't you know?" he asked.

"Do you like me?"

"Yes," he said, wondering where this conversation was leading. "I like you very much."

"Do you like me enough to marry me?"

"I . . . I don't know . . ." he answered truthfully.

"Then, I cannot stay," she said with a smile.

Damn these women, he thought. Always got the hook out for a man.

"You mean, if I say I like you enough to marry you, then you'll stay here with me?" he asked. "I could lie to you. Then, what would you do?" That ought to take some of the wind out of her sails.

She shook her head. "No, you would not lie, especially about a thing like this. I see you every day for six months. I know you. I know your heart. You are not the kind of man who tells lies. I never stay with man before, but I will stay with you. But only if we become married."

"Okay," said Hazzard. "I understand what you mean. Will you stay if I say I will marry you?"

"Oh, I will stay," she answered. "But I will not sleep with you, or make love with you. I will kiss you if you want, but we cannot make love with each other."

Hazzard was more confused than ever. "But you just said . . ."

"When you want me for your wife I will make love with you. But if you say this now, I will not believe it. You spoke the truth first when you said you do not know how much you like me, *desho?* Someday maybe you will ask me to marry you. Then, I will be very happy. If you do not ask me, I will wait. If you marry someone other girl, I will be sad."

Hazzard shook his head and a broad grin spread across his face. "Michiko, come here," and she did.

He took her face in his hands and said, "Kiss me," and she did.

Then, he held her out at arm's length. They were too complicated to try and figure out, these lovely Oriental female creatures, and from now on, he was going to stop trying. Take them just the way they are. They're magnificent.

"Come on," he said, grabbing her arm and walking toward the door. "I'll take you home."

It was two o'clock in the morning, and it took them twenty minutes to find a cruising cab. All the way to Ikebukuro he held her hand.

Michiko directed the driver in and out of the usual maze of small streets and finally told him to stop in front of a small alley. When she got out, she turned and squeezed Hazzard's hand. "Good night," she said, and hurried away.

Hazzard told the driver to take him back where he had picked them up, and settled back in the seat to wonder what was happening to Michael Hazzard. He knew why he had asked Michiko up to his apartment, and so did she. He had failed, and she had laid it on the line. The one requirement. Marriage. Well, just like the man said—don't mix business with pleasure.

Marriage. She wanted a husband. She wanted Michael Hazzard. He thought about it. If he married Michiko it would mean coming home every night. No more beer busts. No more parties with the willing girls of Atami and Ito. No more night life. Just coming home to Michiko every night. She would be at the door, throw her arms around his neck, kiss him, and then serve tea. They would take baths together and she would scrub his back. They would eat together. And for the rest of his life, too. No more cold, lonely nights in bed. No more . . . Whoa! Hold up, Hazzard, old buddy! What the devil are you thinking about? You have been doing fine right up to today. Now, suddenly this . . .

Hazzard shook his head and rolled down the window of the taxi to let the cool night air in and revive him. Thank God for good old Greenstreet-Brown. Soon he would be off to Saigon, and if he ever needed a trip, he needed it now.

The cab had stopped and the driver was looking back with a strange expression on his face. It suddenly dawned on Hazzard that the driver had been saying something and they had been stopped for three or four minutes. Hazzard snapped out of his dreaming. They were back where they had started.

He paid the driver and walked up the road to his apartment. He was still thinking about Michiko when he pushed the key toward the lock and a warning bell went off inside his brain. Springing back, he flattened himself against the wall. When the key had touched the lock, the door had moved. It was open now, and it had been locked when they had left.

Reaching instinctively inside his shirt, he suddenly remembered he had left Sam hidden in the bedroom. He was learning lessons in what not to do very fast these days. He made a mental note to kick himself for being stupid and pushed the door open with his toe. He waited and listened. Nothing. Slowly he slid his arm in through the door and flicked on the light. Still nothing.

He squatted down and peered around the edge of the door. No one, but the place was a shambles. He stood and stepped into the room, closing the door softly behind him. He checked each room. Whoever had been there was gone. There must have been two or three of them. No one person could have done all this in such a short time. Hazzard had only been gone about forty-five minutes.

They had ripped up everything. The toothpaste was all over the sink. The soap was in crumbs. All the boxes in the kitchen had been torn open and their contents dumped on the floor. Every book had been leafed through and tossed about. The cushions and furniture had all been cut open and the stuffing was all over the room. Drawers had been spilled. Clothes were thrown in a heap. The mattress on the bed was an unbelievable mess. The only thing they had not done was knock down the walls. What the hell were they after?

The money he had left in the apartment was strewn about on the remains of the mattress. Then he remembered Sam. He went to the closet where he had hidden the revolver, but it was gone. This was one theft he could not report to the police. In fact, if the police caught the thieves with Sam, and they talked, it would be the end of Hazzard's visa.

He glanced down at the money scattered on the bed. But they were not thieves. They had not taken the money. What the devil were they after? His foot hit something hard. Picking a coat up from the floor, he saw Sam. They didn't want money, and they didn't want a gun. He reached inside his shirt and felt the bulge of the beads in the money belt.

"I wonder?" he said aloud.

*   *   *

3.

A BORING TRIP

*H*azzard spent the next day going to the embassies of the countries he would be visiting. The letters Mr. Brown had supplied were like magic keys. Doors opened, people bowed, and visas were stamped in his passport. He bought a few clothes, a new suitcase, and spent the rest of the day in the office with Michiko arranging for bills to be paid. There was still a lot of money left over and he gave her more than enough to take care of herself and keep the office open for another six months. By that time he would certainly be back.

Nothing was said of the night before, and Michiko tried hard not to show her feelings about his leaving, but little tears popped out anyway. Hazzard did not want an emotional scene at the airport, and insisted on saying good-bye at the office. He kissed her quickly, and then sent the sniffling Michiko home early.

The following day, for lack of anything better to do, he went to Haneda International Airport in the morning, had lunch, and then checked in with Civil Air Transport (CAT). His plane left at two fifteen, and he was a little surprised to find he was booked on a propeller-driven aircraft, and not a jet. Though the flight would be longer this way, his arrival in Taipei would give him more than enough time to make connections and board the coastal steamer.

Haneda International Airport was a very boring place in the summer of 1958 for people waiting to board the various planes for world travel. Especially for a foreigner who would not be accustomed to the Japanese habit of trying to bluff their way through by ineffectually copying what they thought were Western ways. Souvenir counters with indifferent, lazy, and somewhat surly clerks. A dining room with bad food and worse service, and Japanese midget-sized furniture sparsely scattered about in the waiting room.

Hazzard took refuge in the small bar that, for some odd Oriental reason, was hidden off in a corner of the dining room. Here, amid the clouds of cigar and cigarette smoke and the smell of stale beer, were two Aloha shirted American tourists with their over-dressed wives. Hazzard could not help but listen to them. It only took a few minutes and he found himself agreeing with the opinion held in most foreign countries—America certainly was a country of loud mouths, women included.

Finishing his Scotch and water, he escaped to the observation deck that overlooked the ramps and runways. He walked along slowly, and when he came to the far end, he glanced at his watch. One forty-five. Time to go. As he turned to walk back, a hand grabbed his arm, and a familiar voice called out.

"Mike-san! " and Michiko stood before him, radiant in a new dress and high heels. She thrust a small bouquet of flowers into his hand as she breathlessly said, "I thought I would not see you."

Hazzard took a long look at this cute little thing who was his office girl. Then, he reached out, grabbed her firmly, and kissed her hard on the mouth.

"Thanks for the flowers. I'll see you when I get back. Bye-bye now, my little Lotus Blossom," and he walked quickly away.

Michiko watched him leave. She was speechless, and highly embarrassed at being kissed in public, but she was also happy, lonely, and very much in love.

Later, as Hazzard boarded the plane, he looked up and there was Michiko, jumping up and down on the observation deck, waving a now wet handkerchief, and so afraid she wouldn't be seen. Hazzard grinned, raised his arm, and waved.

What Hazzard did not see was the dapper form of Mr. Brown standing in the shade a few yards behind the waving crowd. As Hazzard's plane gained speed and left the runway, Chang walked up beside Brown.

"Well, he is on his way," remarked Mr. Brown.

Chang looked up into the sky at the rapidly disappearing aircraft. "Good. All he has to do now is board the boat."

"Is everything else prepared?"

"Yes," replied Chang. "I leave by jet in two hours. I will arrive in Hong Kong three days before Mr. Hazzard. There will be ample time to complete all the other arrangements."

*   *   *

The flight to Taipei was routine, and the steady drone of the engines soon put Hazzard to sleep. He was gently awakened for supper by a shapely Chinese stewardess. He did not really want to eat, but the stewardess was pretty, and the food turned out to be better than expected. The rest of the time he stayed awake and kept the girl running back and forth for Scotch and waters.

The plane landed on schedule, and Hazzard arranged to be taken to Chilung, the port where the Queen Wilhelmina III was taking on cargo.

*   *   *

The ship was a tired relic of the once flourishing coastal trade. Originally, it had been painted white when it had been owned by the Compagnie des Messageries Maritimes under the name of Le Paquebot "Viet-Nam". Now, rust had taken over and turned the old coating of white paint into a splotchy design of yellow, brown, orange, and gray.

The captain was an energetic, sea dog type originally from Australia with the tough sounding name of Rock Gunther. He appeared to be somewhere in his late fifties, but the way he scurried about the ship giving orders to his Chinese crew made him seem much younger.

He was big and tough with a red complexion and matching hair, and the Chinese crew was frightened out of their wits by his booming voice. He was well aware of this, and despite the shabbiness of the ship's appearance, his crew jumped and ran about like sailors on a well-disciplined naval vessel. Hazzard wondered if perhaps the Chinese crew had not secretly named him the Red Devil.

The second day out Hazzard mentioned this and the captain beamed. As always, the best way to reach a man is through his ego, and the captain was no exception.

"That's pretty close," he laughed. "Actually, they call me the Red-headed Dragon. They're just like a bunch of children, and you can be stern with them if you treat them well and compliment them when they do a good job. They're a fine crew, and they work their balls off running this old tub."

There were only two other passengers. An Englishman named Redman, who came equipped with an overdone Oxford accent and was constantly speaking of his military service in Injah and the gentlemanly sport of polo.

The other was Reisenbaum, a rotund biermeister type from Germany who claimed to be in the Orient on a selling mission for his company.

They all ate with the captain in the ship's lounge, and every night after dinner they occupied themselves by playing poker. The captain usually winning the most, and Reisenbaum losing.

Occasionally, Redman would engage Hazzard in conversation. It was strictly one-sided. Though Hazzard tried, he found it almost impossible to understand what Redman was mumbling about, and limited himself to smiles and nods. Redman thought Hazzard to be the most intelligent one on board. No one else would listen to his ideas on Asia, and Hazzard seemed to agree with all his views.

The German's conversation was limited to the ordering of drinks in the lounge and betting on the poker games. He seemed to have been born with a perpetual frown, which gave him the appearance of distrusting everyone but himself.

When the Queen Wilhelmina III finally reached Hong Kong, she was only twenty hours late. This seemed to please the captain.

"Last time, we were thirty-four hours behind schedule," he boasted.

The others went ashore, but Hazzard, having no business there and not wanting to buy anything, decided to remain on board. The ship would unload cotton waste and take on other cargo in the morning. The sailing time was not definitely set, and Hazzard could not afford to miss the ship.

The next day, Hazzard busied himself watching the crew load packing cases in the hold. The cargo was brought up from lighters that surrounded the ship like worker bees around their queen. Each of the small barge-like boats was also the home of its crew. Children played on the small decks, garbage and latrine swill was tossed over the side, and washing fluttered between the small masts.

In the evening, just before dinner, Redman and Reisenbaum came back on board loaded down with many bags and boxes.

The captain grinned broadly when he saw them struggling up the rickety gangway that led down to the water's edge.

"Look at that," he said to Hazzard. "Things are just so damned cheap, you can't afford not to buy 'em."

For a change, there was no poker game. Reisenbaum and Redman were too tired from their hurried shopping. After a few drinks, everyone went to bed early for a change.

Hazzard tried to sleep, but he was still awake when the ship began to move out of the harbor in the early morning.

When Hazzard came into the lounge, where the others were eating breakfast, there was no land in sight. The sea was calm and reflected the burning sun like a mirror. Even the breeze created by the motion of the ship was hot and dry. Each day, the weather was becoming warmer than the last.

On the third day out, the captain asked for everyone's passport. "We will be running in Chinese territorial waters fairly soon, and we might meet up with one of their patrol boats. And rather than have them asking any of you a bunch of illogical questions, I can take care of everything if I have your passports in my possession," he told them.

Everyone thought the captain knew what he was doing and handed over their passports without any argument.

In the late afternoon, Hazzard had gone up to the bridge to give the captain his passport and had stayed to listen to some of the more interesting tales of running a ship in the South China Sea. Just before dusk, they sighted land on the horizon, and the ship seemed to be steaming directly toward it.

"Are we getting to Viet Nam already?" asked Hazzard.

"No," replied the captain. "Those lights you see on the left, that's the island of Hainan. Over on the right is Kwangtung. Both of 'em are part of mainland China."

"Mainland China?" said an incredulous Hazzard. "You said we would be running in Chinese waters, but his is a lot closer than just being in their waters. Why are we going there?"

"We are not going there, Mr. Hazzard. We are going to sail through the Kiungchow Strait, between the island and the mainland, to get to the Gulf of Tonkin. It's the shortest route to Viet Nam. A Chinese patrol boat will be coming out to meet us, to sort of guide us through the strait. They always do."

"But we're not just in their territorial waters. We'll only be a couple of miles from their shore. They've got a history of capturing boats that come this close and interning the crew and all the passengers . . ."

The captain shook his head. "No, they're quite used to me and this old tub. Been doing this route for some time now. Since way before they started getting nasty about strangers. My radio operator spoke to them about an hour ago."

"These people are very unpredictable. What if they start searching the ship. . . ?"

The captain held up his hand. "I haven't told you the whole drill yet," and he paused to light his pipe. It took three matches before he was satisfied with the billowing clouds of aromatic smoke.

"They'll come alongside and put two or three of them aboard," he continued. "One will take over from my helmsman while the others will go over the passports and make a lot of notes in a big ledger they always carry with them."

"That's all? They don't inspect the cargo, the passengers, or anything?"

The captain shrugged. "To be honest with you, Mr. Hazzard, you never can tell just what they will do. Two years ago they made me heave to for four hours while they went over the whole ship."

"Two men did all that in four hours?"

"Nope. That time it was a whole company of Chinese Marines."

"And what happened?"

"Nothing. It was just a wasted four hours."

"What do you think they were looking for?"

"I think their commanding officer was looking for a handout."

"A bribe?"

"Guess you could call it that. I didn't realize it at first. We just sat in my cabin drinking tea for four hours. I was getting tired of all the fuss his men were making and decided to have a shot of whisky. When that officer saw the bottle, his whole attitude changed. I offered him a drink, and when I saw how much he really liked Scotch whisky, I caught on right away. I had one of my boys bring up a whole case for him, and that was the end of the search. Nowadays, I'm always ready for 'em," and he pointed to a wooden case of Scotch whisky in the corner of the wheelhouse.

"And, Mr. Hazzard," he continued. "I'm afraid I'm going to have to ask you to stay in your cabin until the Chinese have left the ship. If they see any of the passengers, they always start asking a lot of embarrassing questions."

"I've got nothing to be afraid of," Hazzard told him.

"How do I know that?" The captain pointed to the small pile of passports on the chart table. "You have an American passport, and that's enough to start them off if they should happen to see you."

"A few questions wouldn't bother me. I could handle that easy enough."

"If one of them decided he didn't like you or any of your answers, he might say you were a spy and take you off the ship. That could possibly be the last anyone ever heard of you."

"How could they get away with that?" But even as he said it, Hazzard knew they could very easily do it.

"We happen to be in Chinese territorial waters. That's how they could get away with it."

"Okay. I'll stay in my cabin until tomorrow." Hazzard started for the door and paused briefly as he glanced down at the chart table. The top passport was red with gold embossed script and a large crest. "That's a North Vietnamese passport. I didn't think any of your crew could travel to South Viet Nam with that kind of passport."

"It doesn't belong to any of my crew."

"You mean it belongs to a passenger?"

"Mr. Hazzard, in my business I have learned never to ask anyone any questions about themselves. People pay me for a boat ride, and that's just what they get. I don't ask questions, and I don't answer them," he paused to look out the window. "I see the patrol boat coming up, so you'd better be getting below to your cabin."

Hazzard looked at the captain for a moment. Then he nodded and left without a word. He didn't want to become involved with the Chinese. The thought of being taken off the ship and held ashore didn't appeal to him, and he had a few more days aboard the Queen Wilhelmina III to ponder the presence of the North Vietnamese passport.

He returned to his cabin, locked the door, turned off the light, and stretched out on the bunk. He heard the scraping and banging of people coming aboard from the patrol boat and a few shouts in Chinese, just before he drifted off to sleep.

When Hazzard woke up the next morning, the ship had already passed through the Strait of Kiungchow, and the Chinese patrol boat was long gone. As they were eating breakfast, the last faint image of Hainan Island disappeared in the early morning mist.

That evening, they sighted land on the horizon again, and the ship turned south to run parallel with the outline of the distant, hazy shore. It was the coast of Indochina, and the captain told them from now on they would see land every day until the ship reached Saigon.

"If that's Indochina," ventured Hazzard as he and the captain leaned on the ship's rail together and looked across the blue sea. "It must be Viet Nam."

"Yes," replied the captain. "It's the old area of Tonkin. It's called Viet Nam now. North Viet Nam."

Hazzard gazed at the distant gray line of land and wondered about the people living there under the rule of their communist masters. He was glad it was not his destination. But Hazzard had forgotten an old Oriental proverb that said, "The future is not ours to see."

After supper, they sat in the lounge playing poker. Hazzard was sitting with his back to the door that led out on deck, and did not see or hear the newcomer enter.

The captain was the first one to notice, and they all looked up as he said, "Oh, good evening, Mr. Chang. Feeling better?"

"Yes," replied Chang. "Much better, thank you."

Hazzard tried not to show the searching interest on his face. The man called Chang must be the owner of the North Vietnamese passport, and somewhere in the back of his mind he had the uneasy feeling he had known this tall, lean Oriental before. The name and the high cheekbones suggested a heritage of northern

China, but the strange, piercing look in his eyes, seemed to bore through your skull and read your mind, suggested something else. It was the look of a man who could be either a deadly, merciless enemy, or one who could be trusted beyond question with your life. It was a face one would find difficult to forget, and Hazzard finally decided he had never met the man before. Yet, there was something familiar, and as the captain continued to speak, Hazzard filed the thoughts away for further reference.

"This is Mr. Chang," the captain explained. "He came aboard in Hong Kong. He hasn't been feeling too well and has been staying in his cabin." He looked at Chang and pointed to the cards on the table. "Care to join us? There's room for a fifth."

"I would be very happy to play," said Chang. He swung his gaze around the table and stopped for a second to study Hazzard. "If it is all right with everyone else," he added.

"Sure thing," said Hazzard. "Sit down. But I warn you, the captain is extremely lucky tonight. He's been winning all the big ones."

The captain beamed at this. He considered his knowledge of poker to be second only to his knowledge of the sea. Chang sat, and the captain introduced the others, one by one. Reisenbaum was last, and the delay was almost too much for the robust German.

"Ja, ja, und deal da carts," he grumbled.

They resumed the game and the captain won steadily. It was very late when Hazzard, Redman, and Chang threw in their hands, and the captain looked at Reisenbaum, saying, "I'll see your bet Mr. Reisenbaum, and raise."

The color of Reisenbaum's face began to turn scarlet. He fumbled with his money for a moment, and then shoved it all into the center of the table.

"Und I raise," he snapped.

The captain put his cards on the table, reached out and counted the money Reisenbaum had pushed forward.

"All right, I'll just call this time," and the captain placed his money in front of him. "What do you have?"

Reisenbaum slowly turned over his cards. He had three queens. "That's a very nice hand," grinned the captain. "But not quite good enough," and he turned over three cards. All kings.

Reisenbaum could not control his rage. He snorted, kicked his chair back as he stood, and stomped out of the lounge.

"Well," said Hazzard. "That just about cleans me out for tonight."

"Yes," said Redman as he rose from his seat. "I think it is about time for me to get a good night's sleep. If you gentlemen will excuse me," and he strode off stiff-necked to the door.

The captain was busy counting his winnings as Hazzard got up and left the table without a word. He walked up to the small bar in the corner of the lounge and tapped the sleeping Chinese boy on the shoulder.

"How about a Scotch and water, okay?" he said.

"Okey, okey, Scotchy water, okey, okey," came the singsong reply as the boy jumped up and began rattling bottles about in his search for Scotch.

"Mind if I join you?" said the voice of Chang.

Hazzard turned around to face him. "Not at all."

Chang looked at the Chinese boy. "One more Scotch and water."

"Okey, okey, Scotchy water, okey, okey," grinned the boy.

At the sound of Chang's voice, Hazzard had felt that same uneasy feeling again. There was something familiar about Chang. Whatever it was, it was not pleasant. Chang had gotten on in Hong Kong. That was four days ago. Sick in his cabin, the captain had said. But how had Hazzard missed seeing Chang when he had come aboard.

"So, you came aboard in Hong Kong, " said Hazzard, trying to be friendly. "It's strange I haven't seen you before this."

"I came aboard early in the morning, just before the ship sailed, and I have stayed in my cabin until tonight," Chang explained. "I do not particularly like sea voyages, but I find them necessary at times."

"Then why don't you fly?" suggested Hazzard. "This is a real slow way to travel. Why do you find it necessary to travel on this crummy ship, Mr. Chang?"

The boy placed the drinks on the bar, and Chang raised his glass to Hazzard. The drink was warm without ice, and after a small sip, Chang set it back on the bar.

"I am a merchant, and I find it convenient to travel with my merchandise," Chang told him. "I have quite a sizable cargo on board."

"Looks like you don't trust anyone," observed Hazzard. "If you have to ride around with all your stuff."

Chang smiled at this. "And you, Mr. Hazzard. Do you trust everyone? And since we are both being curious, what excuse do you have for traveling on this, as you say, crummy ship?"

Hazzard downed the last of his drink. "I like the sea air, and it's more exciting traveling by ship."

"Yes, Mr. Hazzard, I quite agree with you, and you never can tell just how exciting it will become," and Chang bowed slightly as he turned and walked away.

Hazzard watched as Chang left the lounge. The ship was full of characters, and he smiled as he thought maybe the others were thinking the same about him. He had the boy make him another Scotch and water. Surprising how much a warm Scotch and water tasted like medicine. He gave up the idea of having a third drink and returned to his cabin.

It was another suffocating night. The small electric fan over his bunk breathed a steady stream of hot air over his body. He tried to lie still and think of snow storms he had seen when he was a boy.

*   *   *

4.

THE HOSTAGE

Morning came, and Hazzard lay half naked on his bunk, his eyes shut, sweat running down his sides in tiny rivers, debating whether he could stand another shower of smelly sea water. He had just made up his mind not to move when a deadly silence engulfed the ship.

The engines had stopped, and the steady vibrations that fill a moving ship were suddenly gone. Hazzard opened his eyes. The electric fan above his head was revolving slowly to a halt. He listened carefully and only the faraway sound of water lapping at the sides of the freighter came to his ears.

All his senses snapped alert. He felt a chill surge through his body like an electric shock. This feeling he had known before. He knew the meaning. Something bad was about to happen.

Standing up, he peered cautiously through the open port hole above his bunk. Nothing but the empty deck, the sun, the sea, and silence.

Hazzard remained motionless and waited. One minute, the water splashed lightly at the rusted plates. Two minutes, a sea gull screamed above the ship. Three minutes, the sound of someone walking on the deck outside his cabin. Hazzard lowered himself below the level of the port hole. When the footsteps had passed, he slowly raised his head and looked out again. One of the ship's crew was walking forward with his hands clasped behind his head. Behind him were two heavily armed Orientals with rifles pointed at his back.

Hazzard quickly slipped into his trousers and shoes, grabbed the money belt off the bunk and strapped it around his waist. Taking Sam from beneath the pillow, he checked the revolver, stuck it under the money belt, and put on his shirt.

He had just finished with the last button when there was a knock on the door.

"Who is it?" Hazzard called out.

"Captain want see you Misser Hazzard. He say you come bridge," said a singsong Chinese voice.

"All right," said Hazzard. "Be right with you," and he buckled his belt.

Picking up the small leather pouch of .38 rounds he slipped it into his pants pocket. Then, quietly, he stepped to the door, and in one motion unlatched and swung it open. Almost immediately a tough-looking Chinese sprang into the room with a wicked-looking automatic rifle.

Tripping the Chinese with his foot, Hazzard brought the edge of his right hand down behind the man's ear in a vicious karate chop. The Chinese slammed spread eagle to the floor and lay motionless. Hazzard reached over to pick up the automatic rifle, then froze at the sound of Chang's voice.

"As you can see, these sea voyages get more exciting every day."

Chang was standing in the doorway holding a pistol and smiling pleasantly. Glancing down, he nodded approvingly.

"Very efficiently executed, Mr. Hazzard. It is a pity though. I had hoped to avoid bloodshed. I suppose the death of one or two men is to be expected. Someday we must compare notes on the deadly art of karate." He looked up at Hazzard. "Now, would you care to accompany me to the bridge? We must not keep the good captain waiting."

"I don't see where I have much of a choice."

"Come, come, Mr. Hazzard, not so bitter," smiled Chang. "I assure you, nothing is going to happen to you . . . if you do as you are told."

Hazzard shrugged his shoulders and moved toward Chang.

"Stop where you are, Mr. Hazzard, or I shall be forced to place a bullet in your leg. I am an excellent shot. Please do not make me prove it," and Chang moved slowly backwards through the door. "I have also spent many years training under a very capable teacher of karate. Now, slowly, come through the door, turn left, and proceed to the bridge. I shall be far enough behind you to prevent any little act of violence you may be contemplating. Please, Mr. Hazzard. We are wasting valuable time."

Chang was proving to be a formidable opponent. Now was not the time, thought Hazzard. Later it would come. It always did. That split second when overconfidence would turn into carelessness. Hazzard turned and walked ahead of Chang.

As they climbed the steel ladder to the flying bridge, Hazzard had a chance to look forward. The deck was crawling with activity. The crew was busily engaged in raising the loading booms and uncovering the hatches under the watchful eyes of a small group of heavily armed Chinese. Then, something clicked in Hazzard's brain. Chinese? He glanced toward the shore. It was now only a little over a mile away. They were laying dead in the water right off the coast of North Viet Nam. These armed men had to be Vietnamese. Then, he remembered the North Vietnamese passport. Pirates! North Vietnamese pirates. Hazzard stopped on the flying bridge and glanced over his shoulder at Chang.

"Inside, please," said Chang, nodding toward the door of the wheelhouse.

The captain was sitting in a chair, furiously puffing away on his pipe. Behind him were two deadpan Orientals, each holding a Garand rifle.

"Well, I see the devils got you too," the captain said bitterly. "It beats me what they're up to, but you can bet it won't be pleasant. I've seen these coastal pirates in action before."

"Please, captain, we are not pirates," said Chang. "Now, just be quiet and relax, and you shall soon be on your way again."

"Where are Redman and the German?" Hazzard asked.

"They are safely locked in their cabins where they cannot get into any mischief. Do not worry about them, they are of no interest to us," answered Chang.

"But I am, huh?" said Hazzard.

Before Chang could answer, a sharp crashing sound echoed through the silent ship.

The captain stiffened in his chair. "What the devil are they doing now?"

"Simply anchoring, my dear captain," explained Chang. "I needn't remind you it would be dangerous to drift around helplessly in these waters."

The captain sat back heavily in his chair. "Bloody heathens," he growled.

Chang ignored the captain's remark. "It is just about time," he said, and turning to one of the guards, he spoke in Vietnamese. "Signal them."

The guard put his rifle against the bulkhead and opened a long wooden box. Hazzard immediately recognized the portable U.S. Army signal lamp. The guard aimed the tube through the window and began to send a series of flashes as he slowly moved it back and forth to sweep the shoreline.

Hazzard moved his eyes away from the signaling guard and studied the shore. Then he quickly glanced about the room. Chang was looking out the window, but the other guard was watching Hazzard intently. No, it was not the time yet. He relaxed and began to watch the shore again.

They all saw the answering flash at the same time. Chang grunted something in Vietnamese, and the guard replaced the signal lamp in the box. Taking the captain's binoculars from the chart table, Chang became absorbed in studying the shoreline.

"Well, captain," he said as he looked through the glasses. "We are right on schedule. It shouldn't be very long now and we shall be leaving you."

Chang handed the glasses to Hazzard. "Would you like to see, Mr. Hazzard? I am sure you will find the view interesting, if not a little exciting."

Taking the binoculars, Hazzard focused them on the distant shore. Coming out from small lagoons among the rocks were fifteen to twenty small, low, fast fishing boats. Each had a large sail ballooning from its mast, and the stiff offshore breeze was pushing them quickly toward the Queen Wilhelmina. Beneath the colorful sails Hazzard could make out the forms of four or five men in each boat. This would give Chang a force of almost a hundred men when the small boats arrived. All armed to the teeth, and all of them ruthless, emotionless killers. If he was going to do anything, it must be done before the small boats reached the ship. At the most, there would be ten minutes left. No more, maybe less.

He handed the glasses back to Chang. "Very pretty," he said, and leaned back against the window. "So what happens now?"

"Now, you remain here and keep the captain company," Chang told him as he nodded his head at the two guards and went out onto the flying bridge to supervise the transfer of cargo. The hatches were now open, and lines trailed down into the hold of the ship from the loading booms.

Hazzard shot a glance over his shoulder to make sure Chang's back was toward the wheelhouse, then turned to study the two guards. One of them had relaxed. He was peering through the forward windows at the activity on the deck below. The time to move could not be delayed much longer. The other guard was standing to Hazzard's left, his rifle hanging carelessly in the crook of his elbow.

The captain seemed to sense the tenseness in Hazzard. "Mr. Hazzard," he said in a low voice. "Don't do anything foolish. To these men, life is nothing. Let them take what they want, and they will soon leave. Resist, and they will kill you as quickly as I would slap a mosquito."

Hazzard smiled at this. He remembered the countless times he had slapped at mosquitoes himself. They usually got away. Slowly, he began to inch his way toward the guard on his left. The distance between them began to narrow. Three feet. The sweat was running down his back and legs from the tensed muscles. Two feet.

The guard jerked his head up. Hazzard reacted instantly. Feigning a look of surprise, he raised his arm and pointed behind the guard. As the guard spun around, Hazzard lunged, snatched the rifle from the man's hands and brought it up in a sweeping vertical butt stroke. The guard tried to dodge, but the stock of the rifle cut across his temple and snapped his head back to crash against the bulkhead.

Hazzard did not wait for the man to hit the floor. He whirled around and leveled the Garand at the surprised guard behind him.

"Shhh . . . ," said Hazzard. The meaning being the same in all languages, the guard remained silent.

Hazzard took the man's rifle, and handing it to the captain, he motioned the guard to squat on the floor. A glance through the window showed him Chang had not moved.

"Watch this one," he told the captain. "I'm going out after Chang. You get ready to get this tub underway the second the anchor starts coming up."

"But . . ."

"No buts—do what I say!" Hazzard looked toward the shore and the small boats. "We've only got about four minutes left."

Then leaning the Garand against the bulkhead, he put his hand inside his shirt, quietly opened the door, and slipped out onto the flying bridge.

Chang was leaning on the rail watching the approach of the fishing boats as Hazzard moved up beside him. Grabbing Chang's right arm at the elbow in a vise-like grip, he pushed Sam's muzzle into the rib cage of the tall Vietnamese.

"Don't move, and be careful with your breathing," Hazzard told him. "If I feel one tense muscle, I'll blow you in half." Chang relaxed. "Now, Mr. Chang, you do just what I say and we'll get along fine. Tell those flunkies of yours down there to haul up the anchor."

Chang looked coldly into Hazzard's eyes, the hint of a cynical smile at the corners of his mouth. He could feel the revolver pressing against his side, but Chang felt no fear. To him fear was a luxury he had lost years before. This was just another problematic situation rising for a few moments in the path of his life. He had underestimated the resourcefulness and daring of Michael Hazzard. Here, facing him, were the cold slate blue eyes of unrelenting determination. Eyes that held the promise of death.

Calmly, Chang turned to look down at the forward deck. "Take up the anchor!" he called out loudly in English, then turned to stare once more into Hazzard's eyes.

The men on the deck below stopped their work and looked up at the two figures on the flying bridge. Hazzard glanced down and then out over the water at the oncoming boats.

"Tell them to hurry," said Hazzard.

The cynical smile was more noticeable now as Chang called out to the deck below, "Take up the anchor and be quick about it!"

The men on the forward deck remained motionless. Time was fast running out and Hazzard's patience was at an end.

"What's the matter with those damn fools?" Hazzard said angrily. "Don't they understand what you mean?"

Chang smiled. "No, Mr. Hazzard, they do not. Now, give me your gun, before one of my men becomes overly nervous and shoots you in the back."

"Don't try that old gag on me."

Chang looked behind Hazzard and nodded. The muzzle of a rifle came over Hazzard's shoulder and pressed against his temple.

"As you see, Mr. Hazzard, this is not a gag. Now, slowly, give me your gun."

Hazzard released Chang's arm and handed him the revolver.

The time had come and gone. He should have taken the captain's advice and remained in the wheelhouse. Now, he would be lucky if they did not kill him.

"You see, Mr. Hazzard, my men do not take orders from me in English. Now, turn very slowly."

When Hazzard turned, he saw four of Chang's men standing behind him. Through .the window of the wheelhouse he could see the captain. He was now firmly tied to a chair.

"I am afraid you have become too much of a problem for me," said Chang. "And now I am forced to take rather drastic measures to ensure you do not remain a problem." Then Chang spoke rapidly in Vietnamese to the guards.

The man standing next to Hazzard brought his rifle up quickly and rapped the barrel across Hazzard's skull before he could move. Chang looked down at the unconscious form and shook his head.

"Tie him up," he told the guards and went back to the rail as the fishing boats began to come alongside and tie up to the freighter.

Soon the noise of the winches and the shouting voices of the men filled the ship as crate after crate was hoisted from the hold and lowered into the waiting boats.

The unloading was almost finished when Chang went back into the wheelhouse, where the captain sat red-faced in the chair, fidgeting with the ropes.

"Allow me," said Chang as he untied the knots and threw the rope to one side. "Sorry to have delayed you, captain, but now you may start on your voyage again. And to ensure you will not do too much talking when you arrive in Saigon, we are taking the reckless Mr. Hazzard with us as a hostage."

"What do you mean, talking?" snapped the captain. "How do you expect me to keep my crew quiet? Everyone of them will be jabbering like idiots when we reach port. You're making an impossible demand by taking Mr. Hazzard as a hostage."

"My dear captain," smiled Chang. "I am not worried about your illiterate crew of wharf rats. It is you who must make out the written reports. It is you who will be interviewed by the police and the media. Of course you cannot keep this incident quiet. All I am asking you to do, is to say it happened one hundred miles north of this actual spot. That is all. The rest you can tell. Who knows, you may even write a book about it someday and become rich?"

"And what becomes of Mr. Hazzard?" the captain asked.

"In about thirty days," said Chang. "He will turn up in Saigon or Singapore, in excellent health."

The captain looked slyly at Chang. "And what's there to keep me from telling the correct location then?"

"In thirty days, my dear captain, the location of today's little affair will not make the slightest difference to anyone."

Chang walked to the door, then stopping, he turned around and bowed politely. "Good-bye, captain. And if you should happen to write a book, I hope you will mention my name. People usually call me The Cobra."

The captain stared for a long time at the door through which Chang had disappeared. A cold sweat formed on the palms of his hands. It was the reaction that comes after a man shakes hands with death and lives to tell of it. The captain had heard the name of The Cobra before, but always in hushed tones and whispers. No one wanted to talk long about The Cobra, and most people did not even want to listen. The less you knew about The Cobra, the better. The captain had never heard anything specific. Being a foreigner, the Orientals would never talk freely to him, or in his presence, about this mysterious figure, who was fast becoming a legend in Southeast Asia. The only thing he did know was that the name of The Cobra was linked to one subject—sudden death!

Chang stood on the bow of one of the small fishing boats watching a cargo net lower the bound form of Hazzard. Two well-muscled Orientals gently lifted Hazzard's limp body and placed him on the deck near the mast of the boat.

The last crate had been loaded, and now they were ready to leave.

"Cast off!" Chang shouted in Vietnamese.

Armed men heaved themselves over the side of the larger vessel and slid down ropes to the small sailboats. Hawsers were heaved off and ropes cut away as the tiny armada pushed off from the Queen Wilhelmina and turned toward the shore.

If Hazzard had been conscious, he would have been surprised to see six of the Queen Wilhelmina's crew join the armed guards at the last moment and slide down ropes to the waiting fishing boats.

Halfway to shore, Hazzard opened his eyes. The side of his head was throbbing and it took a few minutes for him to regain his memory. Then, as his eyes began to focus, he saw the outline of the Queen Wilhelmina receding in the distance, and suddenly realized where he was. He jerked against the ropes and felt a strong hand on his shoulder. A flat-nosed Oriental, with an ugly scar cut diagonally across the full length of his face, was squatting next to him. The man solemnly shook his head from side to side and pushed Hazzard down on the deck. The man showed no effort, and the strong firmness of the arm surprised Hazzard. He lay back on the deck and watched the bulging sail stretch against the handmade ropes of the boat.

Suddenly the wind shifted. The sail popped like a cannon, and the rough-hewn boom slashed viciously across the deck, just above Hazzard's face. If he had been sitting up, it would have taken his head off. He stretched his head around and saw the flat-nosed man looking at him from the other side of the mast. The man grinned at Hazzard and pointed at the boom. Hazzard grinned back. He understood now why he had been pushed flat on the deck. He pressed his lips together and gritted his teeth. How could he feel gratitude toward this big, burly pirate, when later he might have to kill him in an effort to escape?

Hazzard's train of thought was suddenly jarred as the sail was quickly lowered and lashed to the boom. The crew then began to skull the boat through the now shallow water of a quiet lagoon that curved inland behind the high rocky coast. Hazzard felt the sand grate coarsely along the keel. The boat had stopped. He was dragged roughly to his feet, his ropes cut away, and his arms lashed

firmly behind him at the wrists. Shoving him forward, they indicated he was to jump into the water and wade to shore. He jumped,
stumbled to his knees, and fell face forward in the water. He came
up gasping for breath. Two guards stood over him, but no one
offered him a hand, and no one laughed. He struggled to his feet,
spit out a mouthful of water, and staggered through the rock-
strewn shallows to the beach.

The two guards pushed him forward to the edge of the jungle.
All around him on the beach, the men were ripping the covers
from the crates. They contained Garand rifles, and 30-caliber light
machine guns. All were packed in waterproof paper that was covered with cosmoline and encased in smaller boxes bearing the sten-
ciled label:

PROPERTY UNITED STATES
ORDNANCE DEPARTMENT.

Hazzard saw Chang checking a machine gun, and when his
guards showed no objection, he walked over to stand beside him.

"Some cargo of merchandise," remarked Hazzard.

"Yes, a very important cargo," replied Chang. "Twenty cases of
rifles, ten machine guns, and five hundred thousand rounds of
ammunition."

"So, you're a gunrunner, or do you just happen to have a sport-
ing goods store somewhere in the jungle?" said Hazzard, in a sarcastic mood.

"I have been called many things, and the name gunrunner is
not new," commented Chang as he continued inspecting the machine gun.

Chang's calm attitude was beginning to eat into Hazzard's
guts. He could not keep the bitterness and loathing down as his
voice lashed out. "You're a real busy boy, Chang. What else do you
do besides being a pirate, kidnapper, and gunrunner? Smuggling?
Murder? Dope? Maybe a little white slavery, or do they call it
something different down here?"

Chang got slowly to his feet. His face burning at the insults. His eyes blazed a warning as he stared at Hazzard. A warning that said, you are now nearer to death than you have ever been in your life. Then, as quickly as it had come, it was gone. Chang relaxed, glanced around the beach, and spoke as if Hazzard had never uttered a word.

"From here we must travel by foot. We break down the loads so they can be easily carried on the shoulders."

"I'm not interested in how you run your band of cutthroats," retorted Hazzard.

"But you will be, Mr. Hazzard," said Chang, and his dark piercing eyes flashed with secret amusement. "And by the way, let me caution you. Many of the men speak a little English I do not think they would take it kindly if they heard you call them cutthroats. Now, if you will excuse me, there is much to be done. Gunrunning is not a simple business."

$$* \quad * \quad *$$

5.

THE GUNRUNNING BUSINESS

The trail through the jungle was a trail in name only. Four men had to proceed ahead of the column to clear away fast-growing vines, bamboo and undergrowth with machetes. Behind them a force of almost a hundred men labored under the combined weight of their weapons and of the new rifles, machine guns, and ammunition. Hazzard carried nothing, yet his bound arms caused him to stumble frequently, and prevented him from slapping at the swarms of insects swooping down upon the sweat-salted bodies moving slowly through the jungle.

The men around him walked in silence, the sweat streaming down their faces and soaking their clothes. These were men as accustomed to the jungle as the big city commuter is to the morning train. Though they looked like a band of down-at-the-heel pirates, Hazzard knew they were dressed to protect themselves against the effects of both the heat and the insects. Their clothing carefully picked to blend with the jungle foliage.

As he watched them move steadily and soundlessly through the jungle, Hazzard began to realize these men were more than

just pirates. They were experienced jungle fighters. A band of efficient, cold-blooded guerrillas. The thought was not pleasant. What
would he find at the end of the journey?

He slipped again and glanced down at his low cut oxfords.
The salt water and the constant slashing of the sharp rocks and
roots along the trail had almost destroyed them completely. His
shirt was slowly turning to rags, and his trousers were mud caked
and ripped.

Every two hours they halted. The men rested by squatting
down and using a stick to prop up the A-frame-style back packs to
take the weight from their shoulders. Hazzard had seen Orientals
relax in this position from Manchuria to Borneo, and never failed
to wonder at the stamina of these people. He knew in five minutes
they would be ready to start out again, uncomplaining.

Eight hours after leaving the beach they came to a slow-mov-
ing, muddy river. Canoes that had been hidden previously in the
thick undergrowth were dragged to the water's edge and loaded
with men and equipment.

Just as Hazzard was trying to maneuver himself into a canoe,
Chang came up and quickly drew a long, shiny dagger. Hazzard
braced himself. Was this how he would die? Stuck like a pig in an
unknown jungle?

Chang smiled as he read the question in Hazzard's eyes. He
grabbed Hazzard by the arm, swung him around, and slashed the
rope away from his wrists.

"Just in case you fall in the water. You can swim better this
way," and Chang waded into the river to swing himself lightly
into the bow of a canoe.

One of Hazzard's guards poked him in the back with a rifle
and motioned him to climb into the long, narrow boat. The canoes were pushed out into the middle of the river, and they started
downstream in single file. Each canoe carried six men. Four to
paddle and two men with automatic rifles to scan the jungle.

When night came they were camped in a clearing by the river.
The canoes had been pulled ashore, campfires lit, and the men

began to talk and laugh in louder than usual voices. From the relaxed security, Hazzard guessed they were now in, or close to, their territory, and the danger of attack had been reduced to a minimum.

His hands remained untied, but across the fire from him squatted his two alert, never-tiring, poker-faced guards. They had given him a crudely made wooden bowl full of half-cooked rice, vegetables, and fish. It was smelly and sour tasting, but to Hazzard, who had tasted nothing since the night before on the Queen Wilhelmina, it was one of the best meals he had ever eaten.

He had just shoved the last of it into his mouth with a pair of well-worn chopsticks when Chang stepped into the light of the fire and squatted down beside him.

Chang poked at the fire with a stick and spoke without looking at Hazzard. "I hope you enjoyed your meal. It is not as tasty as chili con carne, but very nourishing," said Chang.

Hazzard started. How could Chang possibly know one of his favorite foods was chili con carne? Was it just a lucky guess, or did Chang know more than he should about Michael Hazzard?

"Now, I must ask you to give me your parole, and not try to escape," continued Chang. "You could never make it through the jungle alone anyway, especially at night."

"And if I refuse?" said Hazzard.

"Then I am afraid we shall have to tie you up again," and Chang waited patiently for Hazzard's answer.

As if to convince him, a mosquito drilled into Hazzard's neck. He slapped at it and wiped the small smudge of blood on his shirt. A night in the jungle with your hands tied would be a nightmare of mosquitoes coming to the shackled feast.

"All right, but just for tonight," decided Hazzard. "Tomorrow's a different story."

"Of course, Mr. Hazzard, just for tonight," and Chang motioned to the two poker-faced guards.

Hazzard watched with interest as the two men stood and walked away to disappear in the darkness of the trees.

"Aren't you taking chances?" and Hazzard nodded in the direction the guards had taken. "Sending your boys away like that?"

Chang stood up. "You gave me your word, Mr. Hazzard, remember? And if a man's word of honor is not to be trusted," he smiled slightly, "he might as well be dead."

Hazzard looked up, but Chang was gone, leaving him alone by the fire with his thoughts. Chang was right. He could never get through the jungle by himself. Without even knowing where he was, to sneak away would be fatal. They probably would not even bother to look for him. About the only thing Hazzard did know was that he was in North Viet Nam—communist territory. This caused his thoughts to run in a new direction. Who were the guns destined for? Which side was Chang on? Or maybe he was one of those who played both ends against the middle.

Hazzard picked up a smelly rag one of the men had dropped, and lying back, he draped it over his face. Nothing to do now but rest and wait. Tomorrow would hold the answers to many questions.

*   *   *

The following morning they continued downstream. Three hours later Hazzard began to hear the distant roar of a heavy surf, and realized they were again approaching the sea.

The canoes were beached in a much-used and well-guarded clearing by the river. The men shouldered their heavy loads and the party started down a well-traveled path toward the ever increasing sound of pounding waves.

They came out at the mouth of the river where it cut through the towering cliffs to the sea. Turning south they picked their way along the rocky shore at the base of the sheer rock cliffs, the salt spray from the waves drenching their already sweat-soaked bodies.

The rocky path cut quickly inland, and Hazzard saw they were entering a deep, quiet lagoon that nature had formed in the cliffs. The lagoon widened, and they were walking along an ancient stone wharf that fishermen of some forgotten era had painstakingly constructed. Small boats of various shapes and sizes were moored in the quiet waters, all of them equipped with engines as well as sails. Five armed, motorized sampans were drawn up to the wharf and were undergoing overhauls and repairs. As Hazzard walked past them he noticed the inner sides of the gunwales were lined with armor plates. These boats, properly manned, could be very deadly in small hit and run raids along the coast.

The men were now climbing a wide, sloping trail that ran up from the edge of the wharf to the top of the cliffs. At the top, Hazzard turned around and realized the lagoon would be impossible to detect from the sea. Reluctantly, he found himself approving the selection of the site for a base of operations.

From the edge of the cliff the ground sloped away across a large cleared space and stopped abruptly where the jungle formed a green wall of vegetation. He did not really know what he had expected to find at the end of the journey, but a rough, rum-drinking band of brawling men in a cave would not have surprised him. Now, as he gazed on the scene unfolding before him, he was filled with awe.

Stretching out across the flat, cleared area was a well-kept and disciplined community. Children playing, dogs barking, women making flour, washing, weaving, men marching in orderly ranks, clean houses set in neat rows. Any place else in the world and he would not have looked twice, but after his experiences of the last two days, and now being out in the middle of nowhere—it was astonishing.

Hazzard's impression of Chang and his organization was changing. You could not help but admire a man who could build a well-run fighting force from nothing, and keep his base of operations as orderly as any military headquarters in the world. Hazzard now wanted to know more about this group of men who lived in the jungle, smuggled guns, acted like guerrillas and pirates, but operated with the efficiency of a well-organized military unit.

If it were not for the delivery of the beads—but this was impossible. He had to escape and reach Saigon. It could not be much of a run down the coast, especially in one of those motorized sampans. If he could handle one of them by himself—and if he could manage to elude his guards long enough to get his hands on one. For reassurance he pressed his hand against his waist and felt the comforting bulge of the small circle of beads that remained in the money belt.

Then, as the column passed close to the edge of the village, Hazzard was struck by a pathetic scene. In contrast to the orderliness and cleanliness he had first observed was a group of people encamped in the open ground bordering the jungle. Families living in makeshift shelters, their clothes ragged and filthy. Children with skin diseases. The emaciated forms of sick oldsters. Women with drawn faces and sunken chests, and many of them visibly crawling with lice.

Hazzard felt the pit of his stomach tighten at the sight. They looked up at him through blank eyes. The expression of people who have lost all hope, and now waited and wished for death.

Tearing his eyes away from the gruesome scene, he forced himself to stare straight ahead. He noticed the other men in the column paid no attention to these hapless forms of life that lay clustered by the path. Hazzard cursed himself for having had admiration for Chang. He could see now that the tall Oriental was no better than the ancient, bloodthirsty war lords of China. Build an efficient fighting force, keep the soldiers happy—and crush all else that stands in the way. The code of the demented, power-mad dictator.

They had reached the compound in the center of the village, and as Hazzard brought his angry thoughts back to reality, he realized only Chang and the two guards remained. The others had disappeared among the various buildings.

Chang's voice broke through Hazzard's thoughts. "Mr. Hazzard, will you please come with me? And if you will give me your word not to try and escape, we will not need the guards."

"Look, Chang," Hazzard almost shouted. "I can't go on giving you my word about not escaping forever . . ."

"I quite agree with you," Chang told him. "All I ask is for you to give me one hour of your time. After that, if you wish to leave, I will be happy to have you escorted to any place you desire, where you can secure transportation to resume your journey."

If Chang had nothing else, he certainly had gall.

"Well, Mr. Hazzard. Will you give me one hour?"

One hour? Hazzard forced himself to relax and regain control of his emotions. Slapped with a rifle, kidnapped, trussed up like a carcass of beef, almost drowned, forced to walk through the jungle like a prisoner on a chain gang, and now—was it to be a social tête-á-tête, or the Chinese boot? One hour? What the hell.. .

"Okay, one hour," Hazzard said belligerently.

Chang motioned to the two guards, and then they were alone.

"Follow me," said Chang as he turned and walked rapidly away through the village.

Hazzard let out a deep breath, and resigning himself to his not-always-present guardian angel, he followed.

*   *   *

6.
TO CATCH A SPY

*T*hey came out of the village and walked toward the edge of the high coastal cliffs about a half mile north of the lagoon. Ahead of them was a large, well-built, rich-looking Chinese-style villa. As they approached, Hazzard saw it was heavily guarded by fixed and walking sentries, all armed to the teeth.

The guards recognized Chang and let them pass unchallenged. Two men at the entrance opened the door and stood stiffly at attention as they went inside. Turning right, they went down a long hallway to a large hand-carved wooden door. A tall Oriental, who had been standing with his back to the door, snapped his rifle up across his chest and stepped aside. Chang nodded at the man, opened the door and motioned Hazzard to enter.

The room was lavishly furnished with Chinese items usually found only in museums. To Hazzard, it was overly furnished. Four large tables stood about the room, and everywhere you looked were hand-carved chests, cabinets, and chairs. Porcelain vases, jade figurines, ivory statues, and many silver and gold knickknacks seemed to inhabit every nook and shelf. Hand-sewn tapestries covered the walls, and in one corner stood a massive, seven foot high, inlaid folding screen made of hand-carved teakwood. The side of the room facing south toward the village and the lagoon was completely enclosed with sliding glass doors. To Hazzard it looked like all the treasures of the Ming dynasty had been crammed into one room, even though he could not tell a souvenir cookie jar from a Ming vase.

Chang brought a bottle of sherry and two crystal wine glasses to a small teakwood table and motioned to Hazzard.

"Sit down, Mr. Hazzard, and relax," he said. "I am afraid we have treated you rather badly, and now it is time to give you an explanation."

"Now look, Chang, or whatever your name is," said the still angry Hazzard. "I don't want to sit down. I don't want any explanation. I don't want anything from you. All I want is to get out of here. I've got an important business engagement in Saigon."

"Ah, yes," said Chang as he poured sherry into the two glasses. "Delivering the string of beads."

Hazzard could not hide his surprise, and Chang smiled broadly as he continued. "You were hired by Mr. Brown to take a little string of Buddhist prayer beads to Saigon and give them to Ling Ling Yung. In return you would receive ten thousand dollars. You accepted half in Japanese yen. The other half to be paid to you when—and if—you return to Tokyo."

There it was again—the "if"!

"All right, Charlie Chan," retorted Hazzard. "So besides pirates, you also have an efficient spy system. So what's it got to do with you and me?"

"I am the one who decided Mr. Michael Hazzard would be chosen for this assignment. It was I who had you assaulted near your office, and because you were so efficient in dispatching my two unskilled men, I found it necessary to render you unconscious. I apologize for the rough treatment."

"You chose me?" said an incredulous Hazzard. "And you had

me worked over? And what's this about an assignment? You're not making much sense today."

"Shall we say," Chang explained. "That I had you—what was it? Oh, yes, 'worked over' first, and then chose you afterward. You see, I needed a man who was capable of taking care of himself in surprise situations. I had heard of your impressive record and found it quite hard to believe any one man could have accomplished so much in such a short span of life. I am sorry I doubted your ability, but I must say you have more than passed the test. Now, will you please sit down?"

Hazzard slumped down into a chair and shook his head. "You had me checked out? By who? And what for? Not to deliver a stupid string of beads . . ."

"No, the beads were but a ruse. We had to arrange for you to travel willingly. You needed money, and as suspicious as you might become, delivering a string of beads for ten thousand dollars was something we knew you would most likely accept. Then by planning your itinerary, we placed you on board the same vessel that was carrying a shipment of our arms. You could be taken off the ship at the same time we unloaded the weapons, and brought here. We had planned to do it peacefully, but you created a problem. Explaining the situation to you at the time would have delayed us, and possibly compromised the reason you were being brought here."

"I'm confused," said Hazzard, and he took a mouthful of sherry. "You mean I never was supposed to go to Saigon in the first place? The whole thing was just a frame-up to get me here under false pretenses. Without me, or anyone else knowing about it?"

"Bluntly speaking, yes."

"And I suppose it was you who had my apartment torn apart," commented Hazzard as he remembered the complete mess it had been in. "There wasn't a thing left that could be used again."

"Yes," agreed Chang. "But the ten thousand dollar fee should be enough to compensate for a few pieces of cheap furniture and some old pillows."

Hazzard leaned forward. "All right. So I can buy new furniture, but why did you search my place? What kind of wacky reason have you got for that?"

"You use some very interesting words, Mr. Hazzard," Chang replied. "But we had two so-called wacky reasons. First, to make sure you were carrying out instructions by keeping the beads constantly with you. If we had found them in your apartment, we would have canceled the arrangement and forgotten about the initial payment of five thousand dollars. Secondly, it was necessary to put you on your guard. A crude attempt to warn you of the seriousness of delivering the beads."

"And what about the beads?" asked Hazzard.

"They mean nothing."

"So, the beads mean nothing," and Hazzard shook his head wearily. It was gradually becoming more confusing. "Now, let's go back to the boat, the Queen Wilhelmina. If they were your guns, why holdup the ship like a gang of pirates?"

"To divert suspicion," replied Chang. "There is no other possible way to ship arms here without the enemy discovering our plans in advance."

Hazzard thought about this for a moment. It was like quicksand. The more the man talked, the deeper you went into confusion.

"Just who is your enemy? And what do you want from me?" Hazzard asked.

Chang's attitude changed, and he became very serious. "To explain this I must start at the beginning of a long story. It is not a pretty story, and I hope you will have the patience to listen."

Hazzard finished the sherry and set the glass on the table. "All right. I'll listen."

Chang took a deep breath and sighed as he arranged his thoughts. Then he began.

"At one time, my country was called French Indochina, and this area was known as Tonkin. During the last war, the French forces stationed here were under the command of Vichy France, which was collaborating with Germany. Japan, being an ally of Germany, had also sent troops here."

"When the war was coming to a close, the Japanese thought the French army in Indochina might join DeGaulle's forces. To preempt this possibility, the Japanese suddenly turned on the French units that were stationed here, capturing and executing most of the soldiers."

"After the surrender, at the end of the war, Ho Chi Minh returned to Indochina and installed the Viet Minh in Hanoi under the title of the Democratic Republic of Viet Nam."

"The soldiers of Free France began to arrive here in the summer of 1945. A time when the communists were beginning to reorganize themselves. Then, full-scale war erupted between the French and the Viet Minh at the end of 1946."

Chang paused and a bitter look passed across his face as the memory of those times came flooding back to haunt him.

"The communist leader of the Viet Nam Liberation Army, Vo Nguyen Giap, had trained his troops across the border in southern China and slowly built up an efficient jungle fighting force. The war with the French lasted until 1954, when the French were defeated at Dien Bien Phu."

"One year later the country was divided into two and we established a republic in the south of what was left of our country."

"The Americans have now begun to arrive and train our troops, but it is not enough. Now, the Viet Minh, or the Black Flags as the French called them, are at us again. Like the jackal at the throat of the wounded gazelle. There is nothing left to do but strike back, or all will be lost."

Chang stopped again and looked at Hazzard. "Am I boring you?" he smiled.

"I'm just wondering where all of this is leading," said Hazzard.

Chang nodded and continued. "We organized ourselves into various groups. Some of us, being trained in politics and diplomacy, would fight with words in Geneva and the United Nations, seeking help from whatever source presented itself. Others, like myself, who were trained in the arts of war, would disappear into the jungle to recruit and train men to fight as guerrillas."

"Today, our main objective is harassment. To worry the enemy in his own backyard. Our fighting strength is not very powerful, but our very existence is a deadly threat to the communist propaganda machine and helps prove their filthy Red doctrine a lie."

"We are also the end station for an underground escape route for refugees. From here they are sent south in small boats. You passed some newly arrived ones as we entered the village today. We are sadly lacking in facilities, and there is not much we can do for them here. But the refugee is also one of our weapons. When they reach the Free World, they spread the word of our desperate struggle, and tell firsthand of the despotism and brutality brought to our country by this Red scourge."

As Chang paused for a moment, Hazzard asked a question. "And right now, just where are we?"

"Viet Nam," Chang said quickly. "We are in the part known as North Viet Nam. This village is called Tu-Hao-Tuc."

"That's a very interesting story," said Hazzard. "But I still don't see what it has to do with me."

"Patience, Mr. Hazzard. You have but heard the background. Now, I will bring you up to date. It became necessary for us to recruit men from many different countries. Competent men, with sound military backgrounds, who would come here to this village, train our young men and lead them in small forays along the coast. During the past few years we have had no less than ten of these men here. Strong, fearless men. Today, only two of them are left. In the past four months, eight have died."

"Mercenaries?" interrupted Hazzard.

"Yes," answered Chang. "But I don't think they like to be called by that name."

"And you want me to join you? Help train your men? Is that it?" Hazzard raised his hand. "I'm not a mercenary. . . !"

"No, Mr. Hazzard," replied Chang. "That is not why you were

brought here. Strange as it may seem, we need a detective—or to put it into military terms, we need a counterintelligence agent."

"A detective?" said the surprised Hazzard.

"Yes," and Chang rose and walked to the sliding glass doors that looked out on the village. "Come here, Mr. Hazzard."

As Hazzard came up to him, Chang gestured toward the village. "Somewhere out there is a spy. In the last four months we have sent out nine harassing raids. Each was a death trap for the men involved. The Reds knew we were coming, and were waiting. It was at those times we lost the eight men I told you about." Chang turned to face Hazzard. "I am asking you to find the spy. Our former efficient organization is fraught with suspicion, and morale is at a dangerously low level."

Hazzard shook his head. "Chang, as much as I would like to help you, I don't know if I can or not. First, you'll have to tell me about the activities of this spy of yours. Who you suspect. How he gets the information out. How many people had access to the information. In other words, everything you know."

"That is the difficult part," Chang said wearily. "We know absolutely nothing. We suspect everybody, and yet no one in particular. How the information gets out is a mystery. The information itself is usually common knowledge among the men at least a day before a plan is put into operation. Believe me, Mr. Hazzard, we have tried everything. As a last resort, we asked Mr. Brown in Tokyo to help us. He recommended you."

"Why did you ask Brown?" said Hazzard. "Just who is he?"

"I am sorry, but this is something I cannot tell you. We have the same rules you lived under during your ten years as an intelligence operative for your country. It is called 'the need to know' or 'eyes only', and you do not need to know about Mr. Brown."

Hazzard sat again and gazed out the glass doors in thought. So now they won't say who Brown is. Well, at present, Brown is of no importance. Find the spy. What spy? Who spy? Where spy? Information—only that a spy does exist. Impossible situation? One chance in a million. No evidence. No suspicions as to whom the

spy might be, or how he—or maybe she—operates. How can anyone willingly take an assignment that is ninety-nine point nine
percent doomed to failure from the start? Refuse and go back to
Tokyo? Stay and make a fool of yourself?

"Mr. Hazzard, will you stay and help us find this spy in our
midst?" urged Chang.

"Chang, I'm going to lay my cards on the table. I've been
through things like this before—many times. What you are asking
me to do is almost impossible. Even if I could find out who the
spy is, it could take six months, or six years, or maybe forever."

"But will you try?" pleaded Chang. "We ask no promises. You
can have as much time as you need, and a completely free hand. We
will cooperate with you in any manner you deem necessary. We are
already aware of the difficulties of the task we are asking you to do."

No promises. Completely free hand. Full cooperation. The
intelligence agent's dream. How often in the past had Hazzard
thought how much better he could have done his work if he had
not been constantly hampered by stupid rules and regulations
made by idiots who knew next to nothing of an agent's troubles in
the field? This time there would be no pompous colonel of cavalry
whose only worry was making general. No green infantry officers
thrown in for a quick tour of duty in the intelligence branch. This
is the type of chance you've always wanted, Hazzard old boy. Maybe.

"How do you propose I go about this, if I should decide to do
it?" asked Hazzard. "You can't very well advertise the fact you've
just hired yourself a cloak and dagger snooper."

"You have come here to help train our soldiers," Chang told
him. "This is not strange. You will merely be a newly hired foreign
mercenary."

Hazzard thought of his parachute training for OSS many years
before. The door is open. The wind is tearing at your clothing.
You grip the sides with a strength you have never known before.
The green light goes on. There is a quick tightening of your stomach muscles. Someone slaps you on the shoulder. You're falling,
and there is no return—Geronimo!

Hazzard had the peculiar feeling his stomach muscles were tightening when he suddenly said, "Okay, you win." He was falling, and there was no return. "You now have a secret service. Only don't forget I operate in my own way, and on this one, no guaranteed results. Agreed?"

"Agreed," said Chang with a relieved smile. "Another drink?"

"Yes," and Hazzard held up his glass. "Fill it up. This one I need." And he drained it in one gulp. "By the way, I suppose this Ling Ling Yung character, and the crazy password were also part of the little fairy tale about the beads?"

"No," said Chang. "Ling Ling Yung is very much alive, and the password is real. It was to be used if you doubted my story of why you were brought here."

"All right. Now, the next thing I want to do, is meet this Ling Ling Yung. If we're going to play games, we might as well go all the way."

"Of course," agreed Chang, and his face and eyes lit up with amusement. Then, without taking his eyes off Hazzard, or raising his voice, he said, "Ling Ling, Mr. Hazzard would like to meet you."

Hazzard looked at Chang as though the Vietnamese had just gone completely out of his mind, when suddenly, the massive seven foot high folding screen slammed shut against the wall. Hazzard jumped up in astonishment.

Sitting in a high-backed chair was the most beautiful Oriental woman Hazzard had ever seen. She was not just beauty herself, she was a monument to it. Her facial features appeared to have been carved from the purest tan-colored ivory, each detail a masterpiece of perfection. A smooth molded forehead. Sparkling eyes encased in almond-shaped frames. Eyelashes that swept excitingly like delicate miniature folding fans. A sensitive, finely formed nose with sensual nostrils. Soft moist lips of natural red. A regal chin. Perfectly set jet black hair, and a penetrating look of interest, making Hazzard's senses reel with the same effect you receive from a pipe in an opium den.

Behind her stood a gigantic Chinese. Almost seven feet tall, with an ape-like face, distrustful eyes, ears that were bent and scarred, and thick muscular hands as big as meat platters. He was dressed in a long flowing Chinese gown, and from the size of him, Hazzard guessed he must weigh over three hundred pounds, all bone and muscle. It was this giant of a man, who had slammed the heavy screen to the wall without effort.

As Hazzard turned his stupefied gaze on the woman again, he vaguely heard Chang's voice. "This is Madame Ling Ling Yung. She is the one who controls our group here at Tu-Hao-Tuc. And standing behind the chair is her bodyguard, Ming Lee."

Hazzard heard the words, but this lovely creature sitting there so calmly in the chair defied all description, and he could neither move nor speak.

"Mr. Hazzard," said the throaty voice of Ling Ling Yung. "I am told in your country it is considered impolite to stare."

Hazzard snapped his gaping mouth shut and stumbled for words. "Why I . . . I never expected to find a.. . a woman . . . I mean here . . . in the jungle.. . "

Ling Ling smiled at him. Hazzard thought his knees would melt. "And just what did you expect to find here in the jungle, Mr. Hazzard?" she asked.

Hazzard knew if he opened his mouth again in his present confused state, he was sure to put both feet into it. The next thing he knew, Ling Ling was out of the chair and walking toward him. The long Chinese dress fitted her like a glove, and as she moved, he could see beautifully shaped calves flash by in the slits at the sides.

She stopped directly in front of him and looked up through half-closed lids.

This was about the sexiest look a woman could possibly give a man, and Hazzard had the uneasy feeling she knew it. He had the sudden urge to grab her and crush her mouth in a violent, lustful kiss—the hell with beads, spies, and pirates. The temptation faded as he caught sight of the seven-foot Ming Lee, who now stood right behind her. No wonder she could act sexy, she had all the protection any girl would ever need.

"Now, Mr. Hazzard," she said in a husky whispering voice. "I believe you were paid to bring me something. A small Buddhist rosary. Is it not so?"

Hazzard snapped out of the sex cloud he had been floating on and came back to earth.

"Just a minute," he said. "How do I know you are really Ling Ling Yung?"

"If we are going to play games, we might as well go all the way," she said, mimicking Hazzard's words. "There is terror in the bamboo only for the wicked. Now, may I have the beads?"

Hazzard reached inside his shirt to get the beads. To Ming Lee, who could not understand what was being said, this action appeared to be a threat to Ling Ling, and he started to reach out to defend her. As Hazzard saw the movement and the look in the giant's eyes, he froze.

Ling Ling place her hand lightly on Ming Lee's arm and shook her head. The giant stopped, but continued to regard Hazzard with hostile, suspicious eyes.

That was a close one, thought Hazzard. The big man was amazingly quick for his size, and blindly loyal. He must remember to be very careful of his movements in front of this king-sized bodyguard from now on.

He brought out the beads, held them up in plain view and carefully passed them to Ling Ling.

She took the small string of beads, examined them very carefully, and then said, "Thank you, Mr. Hazzard, for bringing the beads, and thank you for agreeing to help us. We shall forever be in your debt. Now, if you will please excuse me, I know you have many things to talk about with Chang." Then, she turned abruptly and left the room with Ming Lee.

"You have passed the final test," Chang told him as the door closed behind Ling Ling and the giant bodyguard. "If you did not have the beads with you, she would have thought you too careless to be trusted."

Hazzard was still staring at the door. "She's magnificent," he murmured. "Who is she?"

"You are not the first one who has ever said that," replied Chang. "She is the last remaining descendent of one of China's ancient warlords. Her mother and father and the rest of her family were killed by the communists during the war. She managed to escape with some trusted friends and came to live in Viet Nam. When the communists brought war and terror to this country, she decided it was everyone's duty to fight against this Red menace. She organized and equipped a small guerrilla band here at Tu-Hao-Tuc. The people worship her because she has never turned anyone away when they were in trouble. She is a very brave woman, and has devoted her life to one thing—fighting communists. There isn't a person here who would not gladly give up his life to save her."

"Well, you wouldn't need many people to protect her," remarked Hazzard. "If you had two or three more guys around like that Ming Lee character. He doesn't even trust me."

"He trusts no one except Ling Ling and himself," said Chang. "Many years ago Ling Ling's father found Ming Lee in the streets of Peking. A dirty, simple-minded boy. Her father had dropped a packet containing money. Ming Lee picked it up and ran after him to give it back. An unheard of thing among the lower class people who usually went into things like begging and robbery. The honesty of the boy so struck her father that he took him into his house and adopted him. Ling Ling was a very young child at the time, and Ming Lee soon appointed himself her protector. It has been that way ever since. The reason he trusts no one is that Ling Ling's parents were killed after one of the family's closet friends informed on them to the communists. Ming Lee, although simple-minded, realized even a trusted friend could be dangerous. He now believes the safest way is to trust no one, including myself."

"Since we're getting case histories, how do you come to be here?" asked Hazzard.

"While I was organizing the people in the back countries to defend themselves against being forced into the communist guerrilla bands being organized by Giap, Ling Ling sent for me. I have since set up training plans here, and have traveled over most of the world looking for experienced fighting men to come and help us. There is one other thing I will tell you, as you probably will hear it soon enough anyway. People sometimes call me The Cobra."

Hazzard looked puzzled. "The Cobra?"

"Yes," smiled Chang. "It is a myth we have fabricated to help keep the morale of the people up. The vast majority are simple farmers, uneducated, and very superstitious. We have planted the idea that The Cobra has come to avenge them. Every time we stage a raid on the enemy, we circulate the story that The Cobra has struck again. We also give The Cobra credit for any calamity that befalls the Reds. The recent famine in China was even attributed to The Cobra. The people believe it mostly because they want to believe it. Every oppressed people in the world must have something tangible to believe in as a savior. It is not so difficult to understand if you know the basic psychology of the Oriental, and some of our history. In the last war General Chennault practiced this in China with his famous Flying Tigers. Each fighter plane was painted to resemble a shark coming in for the kill. Someone had to be elected to play the living image of The Cobra, and I must tell you that the rumors I hear about myself are sometimes incredible."

"That makes some kind of sense when you think about it," agreed Hazzard. Then, he brushed all this from his mind, and changed the subject back to the present. "Now, about this spy. Where do we go from here?"

"There is nothing more I can tell you. You now know as much about the spy in our midst as we do. Which, I am sorry to say, is nothing. As far as everyone else is concerned, from this moment on, you will be just another mercenary soldier hired by me. Only Ling Ling Yung and I know the real reason you are here. As Ming Lee does not understand a word of English, you need not concern

yourself about him. Now, it is time to take you around and introduce you to the others. The two remaining foreigners and our
doctor, with whom you will be working. Ah, yes, let me add that
no one, including our hired mercenaries, is above suspicion."

Chang rose, started to walk to the door, and paused. "Ah, yes,
I had almost forgotten," and he pulled Sam from his pocket and
handed the pistol to Hazzard. "Your revolver, Mr. Hazzard."

Hazzard grinned as he took Sam. Then, inspecting the revolver quickly, he stuck it inside his shirt under the money belt,
and followed Chang from the room.

*   *   *

7.
THE MERCENARIES

*T*hey left the villa and Chang led the way down a well-worn path that wound inland through the jungle. Hazzard began to hear the hoarse cries of men, and someone shouting in French as they neared the top of a small hill. Before them, in a small clearing, a group of men were training on a bayonet course under the direction of a short, heavy-set, bull-necked foreigner who was screaming at them in French.

A man charged out from the group and attacked a life-sized dummy. The bayonet went in low and was deflected toward the ground.

The booming voice of the Frenchman ricocheted through the trees. "Non, non, non, non!" he screamed in French. "Keep the bayonet up, up, up! If that was a real man, you would now be a young corpse!"

"That is Maurice Paquet," explained Chang. "He was with the underground in France during the Nazi occupation. After the war he joined the French Foreign Legion, which brought him here. When he was discharged in 1951, he came back because he had fallen in love with the country, and put his life savings into a small plantation. He is a hard task master, but his men worship him. "

"Do you trust him?" asked Hazzard.

Chang ignored the question, and went on with the history of the Frenchman. "His plantation was overrun in 1954 and his wife killed by a roving band of the Black Flags. His only son died in his arms in the jungle because the bandits had also destroyed the medical supplies."

"The bandits shot his son?"

"No," replied Chang. "His son suffered from diabetes, and without insulin, the disease is fatal."

"So, you do trust him."

"As I would my own brother," and Chang called out to the Frenchman. "Maurice!"

The Frenchman turned toward them, shouted some orders to his men, and as he came closer, he studied Hazzard with interest.

"Maurice, I would like you to meet Mr. Hazzard," said Chang. "He is a new member of our group."

Extending his hand, Maurice's face broke into a cordial smile. "Ah, welcome to this paradise of the Orient, Monsieur Hazzard."

Hazzard felt the strong friendly grip and a sudden liking for this rough and tumble Frenchman. "My friends call me Mike," he said, looking straight into the unwavering eyes of Maurice.

Maurice liked what he saw in the strong lean lines of Hazzard's face. "Then, I will call you Mike. We shall be friends, non?"

There was a sudden shout from the men, followed by gales of laughter. A young man had just attempted to parry the wooden rifle of a dummy, but had tripped and fallen in such a way that the dummy's rifle had cracked him across the top of the head. He was now sitting on the ground looking very foolish while his comrades laughed and howled.

Maurice shrugged his shoulders in the typical Gallic gesture that covered so many meanings. "Excusé moi, but my children, they need me," and he walked back down the hill.

A mighty shout in French brought instant silence to the area.

Walking up to the clumsy young man, Maurice pulled him roughly to his feet, grabbed the rifle from the man's hands, and sent him reeling back to join his comrades.

Raising the rifle over his head, he lectured them in French. "What is this? This is not a toy! This is a rifle!"

Then Hazzard was initiated to the eccentric teaching methods of the Frenchman. If it had not been for the seriousness of the subject, death by the bayonet, it could have been classified as comic opera. Yet despite the humor, the Frenchman got the point across very clearly.

Maurice pointed delicately toward the muzzle of the rifle.

"This, mes ami, is a bayonet, and when the fight comes— what do you do, eh?"

He approached the dummy on tiptoe, took a comic stance, and bowed.

"You stand, so?"

Then he addressed the dummy.

"Pardonnez moi, monsieur, but your rifle is in my way. Votre permission . . ."

And he pushed the dummy's wooden rifle to one side with his finger.

"Would you mind holding still for just one moment? Merci, you are very kind."

Putting the point of the bayonet against the dummy's chest, he closed his eyes, turned his head away and slowly pushed the bayonet into the dummy.

The change came so fast it was startling, and the smiles of the men disappeared as quickly. Maurice pulled the bayonet from the dummy, and leaping around, he ran back toward the men like a demon from hell.

"Non!" he shouted. "Regarder! Watch me and remember!"

With a screaming war cry, he charged the dummy with a quickness and agility that was amazing. It all happened at once with perfect timing. He was at the dummy, parried the wooden rifle, bayoneted it in the chest, withdrew and followed through with such a powerful vertical upper-butt stroke, the head of the dummy tore off and sailed high into the air.

He came running back to the cowed group of men, threw the rifle to its owner, and standing with his hands on his hips, he shouted, "Like so—proceed!"

And the men ran through the bayonet course with a strength they had never known before. Loud cries on their lips and hate in their hearts for what the dummies represented. The image of the killers who came from the north to pillage, murder and rape.

"He's quite a boy," remarked Hazzard with admiration.

Chang, who was already aware Maurice was 'quite a boy', merely grunted. "Come, Mr. Hazzard. There is still much for you to see."

The path cut through the jungle and angled off toward the sea. Neither spoke, and Hazzard began to take an interest in the colorful birds flitting through the heavy foliage. He was brought back to reality when a machine gun opened fire, and the sudden sound triggered long forgotten reflexes, which threw him head-long into the underbrush.

Chang recognized Hazzard's reaction for what it was and saw no amusement in it.

"I am sorry. I should have warned you," and Chang pointed along the trail ahead of them. "Our practice firing range," he explained.

Hazzard, grumbling incoherently to himself, and brushing dirt and leaves from his clothes, crawled out of the tangled undergrowth. The firing was coming in short bursts with long intervals between, and became louder as they stepped from the trees near the edge of a narrow cove. Ahead of them two machine guns were emplaced in positions covering the opposite bank. About twenty men sat behind the gunners, watching and waiting their turns to fire.

"We have found the sound of firing does not carry out to sea from this location," said Chang.

Just then, a man, who had been bending over a machine gun,

straightened up, and the crew fired a burst across the cove. The man was tall and slim, wore khaki-colored clothing, carried himself with a touch of arrogance, and wore a German Wehrmacht army cap. Hazzard had seen these caps by the thousands when he had been in Europe with OSS, and knew he could not be mistaken.

"Who's the Prussian general?" asked Hazzard.

"That is Heinrich Stürmer," replied Chang. "He was once a colonel in the German army."

"He looks like he still is."

"He is a strange man," confided Chang. "He can speak German, French, English, and Arabic, yet he talks very little, stays to himself, and when he does talk, it is usually something that shows he is bitter at the world."

Chang raised his arm to point. "You see the little man next to Stürmer? That is Moro. Stürmer saved his life once at great risk. Since then, Moro has never been more than a few feet away. He even sleeps outside Stürmer's window. The strangest thing is Stürmer tolerates Moro—and the two of them have never been known to speak with each other.

"Sounds like the real friendly type," said Hazzard.

Stürmer had noticed the two men standing at the edge of the trees and was now walking with slow, deliberate, precise military steps in their direction. Behind him came the short waddling form of Moro. Stürmer stopped in front of Chang, straight as a ramrod, clicked his heels with a stiff military bow of his head, and turned to look intently at Hazzard. His attitude seemed to demand an explanation for the presence of this stranger.

"Herr Stürmer, this is Mr. Hazzard. I have just brought him back with me," and Chang turned to Hazzard. "This is Herr Stürmer."

Stürmer nodded and glanced down at Hazzard's torn shoes. "And you are to be with us?" he asked in clipped English that betrayed no sign of emotion.

"Yes, I guess I am."

"You are an American," said the German.

It was a statement, not a question, and Hazzard could not see what the German was driving at. It might just be friendly conversation, but according to Chang, Stürmer was not one to engage himself in friendly chats.

"Yes, I am," said Hazzard. "Why do you ask?"

"I can tell by your accent," and having satisfied himself he had correctly identified Hazzard's nationality, he turned away. "Now, if you will excuse me," and went back to his men and machine guns.

Walking back along the path to the village, Chang told Hazzard one more interesting fact about the strange family of foreigners he was to work with. A fact Hazzard was soon to see brought into dramatic reality.

"There is something you should know about Stürmer and Maurice," said Chang. "They do not get along very well with each other."

Hazzard lifted an eyebrow. "Oh? What seems to be their problem?"

"They are still fighting the last war. I should say Maurice is the one who wishes to continue it. The French underground against the Nazi. But Stürmer has proven quite capable of handling the situation. So far it has not broken out into actual combat. It just smoulders along waiting for one of them to add enough fuel for an explosion."

The whole situation at this small village of Tu-Hao-Tuc was becoming more complicated with everything Hazzard learned, and becoming more interesting. It was the type of situation that offered endless material for Hazzard's calculating, curious mind.

Back in the village, Chang led Hazzard toward a long L-shaped building with a large red cross painted on its white door.

"This is the hospital," Chang told him with an apologetic tone. "It is not very modern, but it is the best we can do. Come. I want you to meet our Doctor Kelly."

Inside the hospital a few old beds of various shapes and sizes were arranged along both walls, and between them mats and straw mattresses had been laid on the floor to accommodate the overflow of patients. Every space was filled with people lying or sitting. Each a monument to filth and stench. Hazzard gagged at the sight. The rancid smell of sweating humans, dried urine, and medicine filled the heavy air. Everywhere were dirty bandages, and hungry flies buzzing about looking for a filthy place to land and enjoy themselves. There were the amputees, the delirious, the half starved, and the putrid effects of tropical skin disease mixed with gangrene all about him, and Hazzard felt a mixture of pity and disgust. They gained the end of the long room and Hazzard shuddered with relief as they passed through a door and left the appalling scene behind.

They were now in the small room that served as the office of the hospital. It was littered with a variety of small tables, boxes, and shelves containing piles of various medical instruments, books, and bottles of medicine.

Seated at a desk, with his back to the door, was a middle-aged man. Streaks of gray showing in his once brown hair, and with bloodshot blue eyes; his hawk-like nose acting like a pointer, he was absorbed in the mysteries of a medical journal. His arms were outstretched, hands resting on the edge of the desk, and near his right hand was a bottle of unidentifiable whisky and a half-filled glass.

Behind the desk, chained to a bamboo-latticed window, was an extremely dirty and mangy monkey, solemnly picking at a piece of fruit. On the floor about the desk, among the monkey's discarded bits of fruit, lay a profusion of medical books with mildewed covers. To the stranger, it was the headquarters of the local ragpickers society with added smells.

Chang broke the silence. "Doctor Kelly . . ."

"The great Mr. Chang," interrupted the sarcastic voice of Doctor Kelly. "The great legendary figure, The Cobra! Hail the conquering hero!"

"This is Mr. Hazzard, " said the unaffected Chang.

Kelly swung around in the chair and squinted at Hazzard. "Well, don't tell me you found another sucker? Welcome to Shangri-La. What kind of story did you tell this fellow? Fight for freedom? Liberty or death?" He aimed his bloodshot eyes at Hazzard again. "I hope you're healthy, young man. Don't get sick around here. I don't have enough medical supplies to cure a headache." He got up from the chair and walked over for a close look at Hazzard's face. "Son, why did you come here?"

"Because I thought you people could use a little help," said Hazzard.

"To fight the lost cause?" said Kelly bitterly. "Did you see those people out there in this excuse for a hospital? Wounded. Sick. Dying. You'll end up like them, and I won't be able to help you." He jerked his hand toward the window. "But if you're lucky, you'll wind up out there in the jungle with a bullet in your heart, or a knife in your back." His voice rose and trembled as he pointed to Chang. "Ask him, he knows, but he's afraid to tell you. This isn't the shining outpost of freedom he'd like you to believe it is. It's the devil's own gateway to hell." Having worked himself up to a feverish pitch, he now turned his wrath on Chang. "And what did you bring back with you this time? Bullets? Guns? Hand grenades? Or maybe a little poison to take in case they capture us alive?"

"Yes, I brought back guns," Chang replied in a patient voice. "And I also brought back five cases of penicillin."

Kelly's mouth dropped open in astonishment as this statement hit him and instantly dissolved his pent-up anger.

"Why didn't you say so in the first place?" he snapped, and dashed from the room.

"And that, Mr. Hazzard, is our Doctor Kelly," said Chang with a weary smile. "In his sober moments he is rather a good doctor, but I'm afraid the conditions he has to work under have left him a little bitter."

"Well, I can't say I blame him very much," nodded Hazzard as he looked at the litter-filled boxes and shelves.

Chang opened a side door that led directly outside, and Hazzard wondered why they had not used this door, instead of the nerve-torturing walk through the long room of half-dead human wretches. Was Chang trying to prove something? Was the tour past the tragic scene part of his education into the life of the guerrillas? The only thing it had proven to Hazzard was that he would not be able to eat well for a week.

"Come, I'll show you to your quarters," said Chang as they left the hospital.

*   *   *

8.

THE COUNTRY CLUB

The quarters turned out to be a long, low, board building with a thatched roof and a wide bamboo-railed verandah stretching across the front. Inside, a large room ran across the full width of the building. A long table stood in the middle, surrounded by fifteen makeshift bamboo chairs. Along the walls were rough board bookcases, shelves, and an ancient upright piano with a battered military radio receiver on its top. Smaller tables were buried under stacks of old magazines in French, German, English, and Chinese. An old hand-wind phonograph with a pile of cracked records stood on top of a wooden packing crate, and various pieces of crude bamboo furniture were scattered about the room.

On the walls were calendars, pin-ups, and a dart board made from a life-size poster of a nude stripteaser that had once beckoned men into a cheap Saigon theater. Hanging from the ceiling were two naked light bulbs and four kerosene lamps. A few native spears, machetes, and whisky bottles completed the decor.

Despite the roughness and makeshift appearance of the room, Hazzard noticed it was kept clean and dustless.

"This is called the Country Club," said Chang. "You will stay here with Maurice, Stürmer, and the doctor. This is the living room of the quarters, and it is also where you will take your meals."

Chang walked toward a door leading into a hallway, which ran down the center of the building behind the main room. He clapped his hands together loudly. Almost instantly a grinning Oriental appeared in the opening.

"This is Mr. Hazzard," Chang told him in Vietnamese. "He will stay here from now on. You have a room ready?"

The man bowed quickly several times and pointed through the doorway.

"This is Wong, the houseboy," Chang told Hazzard. "He will take care of you."

They followed Wong through the doorway. Hazzard saw that the corridor ran through the center of the building to a door in the rear leading outside. Along each side were seven doors, evenly spaced, indicating this part of the building was divided into fourteen rooms.

Chang pointed to the first door on the right. "This is Doctor Kelly's room," then he indicated the door directly across the hall from Kelly's. "And this is Maurice's room."

"And where is Stürmer's room?" asked Hazzard.

"The last one on the right. He likes to be by himself," replied Chang.

Wong opened the door to a room midway down the right hand side and stood in the hallway grinning at them.

"This will be your room," Chang indicated. "If there is anything you need, just ask Wong. He understands many English words, though he is usually too bashful to answer you. If you have any difficulty, try gestures, he has a very quick mind. Now, I must leave you. I have many things to attend to. Tomorrow I will introduce you to the men you will train. Wong, take good care of Mr. Hazzard."

Wong smiled and bowed rapidly as Chang left, then motioned Hazzard to enter the room. "Wong, do you think you can get me some hot water, a towel, and some soap?" Hazzard asked.

Wong grinned and ran off down the hall. Wondering if the

houseboy had really understood him, Hazzard went into the room and shut the door.

The room was about as big as an ordinary hotel room. A metal cot stood by one wall with a rolled up mosquito netting suspended from the ceiling. A glassless window let light filter in over the crudely hewn wooden floor. A warped chest of drawers stood in one corner. Against the wall by the window, a table stood beneath a cracked mirror. Pasted next to the mirror was a large cut-out French pin-up with her round fat bottom sticking out saucily.

"Why, hello there. My name's Mike," Hazzard said aloud as he patted the rump of the pin-up. "That's what I like. The silent type."

The hair on the back of his neck bristled, and reaching inside his shirt for Sam, he spun around as he sensed the presence of someone in the room behind him. It was Wong. He was standing in the middle of the room, grinning from ear to ear, holding a pan of water, a towel, and a small bar of used soap.

"Oh, it's you, Wong," and as Hazzard relaxed, he pushed Sam back into his waistband. "Thanks for the hot water."

Hazzard glanced behind the houseboy and saw the door was shut. Wong had opened the door, entered, shut the door, and walked to the center of the room without making a sound. It was a weird feeling to know there was someone around who could move that quietly.

Wong placed the pan of water on the table under the mirror. Then stood watching Hazzard expectantly, as though waiting for further orders.

"Wong, who had this room before me?"

Wong giggled his understanding and pointed to the wall by the door. Hazzard had not seen it when he came into the room, but drawn on the wall with colored pencils, was a large American Confederate flag, and carefully printed below it were the words:

SAVE YOUR CONFEDERATE PIASTERS MEN
SOUTH VIET NAM WILL RISE AGAIN
Dan Pierce, Roanoke, Virginia. 12 Oct. '56

Hazzard read the words and thought of the man who had written his defiance of the communists on this wall a million miles from nowhere. Now, he was gone, and no one knew or cared. Is this what we live for, thought Hazzard? To die in a godforsaken hole, forgotten by the rest of the world? How many men had died this way so fat old ladies could go on gossiping over their party lines, and big-mouthed politicians could sit secure in their plush, paid-for-by-the-people offices?

Hazzard shook his head. This was bitterness, and he knew it. Freedom means more than this, and the fight probably would go on forever, dragging the good into premature death and multiplying the opportunities of the profiteers. Someone had to do the killing. Someone had to do the dying. And someone had to do the living. Men like Dan Pierce and himself could not do all three. Hazzard wondered if he was destined to leave the living up to someone else. The ones who did the most living probably did not even appreciate this eternal sacrifice to the God of War, or maybe they didn't even know about it. The safe ones were always too smug to care.

Hazzard sighed wearily. He had to stop thinking like this, and as he turned around he caught a glimpse of himself in the cracked mirror. Reaching up, he felt his chin and realized the three-day growth of beard made him look like a hard case bum.

"Say, Wong, do you have a razor I could borrow?"

Wong's grin melted and he cocked his head to one side.

"You know, razor," and Hazzard made the motions of shaving.

The grin popped out again, and with deft hands Wong reached into the folds of his jacket and whipped out a straight razor. He was holding it up, open, with the blade only inches from Hazzard's face.

Hazzard tensed. The houseboy had gotten the idea, but how eager can you be? Hazzard held out his hand and Wong placed the razor in it. Hazzard relaxed.

"Thank you, Wong."

Wong bowed his grinning face out the door. Hazzard wondered how many more weird characters he was destined to meet before he could say, "Now I've seen everything."

He shut the door and noticed the bolt had been ripped from the wall. It would be impossible to lock the door from the inside. He glanced at the flimsy bamboo strips across the window and decided it did not make any difference. If anyone wanted to get into the room, a locked door would only make them use the window. Hazzard had nothing worth stealing except Sam. But this was like the old story of Mary and the lamb. Everywhere Hazzard went, Sam was sure to go.

He had just finished shaving when he heard the sound of marching troops. Looking out the window, he saw Maurice bring his men to a halt in the compound. The Frenchman was like a mother hen fussing with its chickens. He went down the line straightening a hat here, a rifle there, and when he was finally satisfied, he dismissed them.

Hazzard had noticed the ragtag assortment of weapons. American, British, Russian, and Czechoslovakian rifles, Chinese hand grenades, German pistols, and odd pieces of equipment he had yet to identify. Supplying ammunition for such a variety of rifles would be a tremendous problem.

There was a knock on the door, and Maurice's voice was booming out, "Allo, Mike?"

"Come in, Maurice."

The door swung open and Maurice came in with an armful of clothing. He threw a pair of worn, but still serviceable boots on the floor.

"I notice your shoes today. They are not for the jungle," he said. "Maybe these fit you, non?"

Glancing down, Hazzard saw his oxfords were caked with mud and almost ripped to shreds.

"Maybe these are your size, I think," and Maurice flung a tan shirt, trousers, and an Australian bush hat on the bed.

"Thank you, Maurice, but I don't want to borrow your clothes."

"They are not mine," shrugged the Frenchman. "They were the clothes of Monsieur Dan Pierce, but he does not need them now."

Slowly Hazzard picked up the shirt and looked at it. The clothes of Dan Pierce. First his room, and now his clothes. Was it good luck or bad luck to wear a dead man's shoes?

"They are clean," said Maurice when he saw Hazzard examining the shirt. "No little bugs, no dirt, no blood, nothing."

Hazzard took off his tattered shirt and put on the tan one. The sleeves were a little short, but rolling them above the elbows would take care of that. The rest was fine.

Maurice was leaning against the wall watching Hazzard try on the boots and trousers. This American was a strange one. He had the spark in his eyes that Maurice seldom saw anymore. The spark he had seen so often among his comrades in the resistance. But besides the spark there was something else. A haunted restlessness. It was either the look of a man who had seen too much of life and death, a man who had a keen, probing mind and could look into another man's eyes and read his thoughts—or it was the look of a man who has a terrible secret locked in his heart, forever trying to escape from it, lying awake nights for fear of talking in his sleep. Which one was Michael Hazzard?

"Monsieur Hazzard, why do you come to this place?"

"Chang gave me a good proposition," replied Hazzard. "And I took it. That's why."

"You are a fool," Maurice told him. "But you will find this out for yourself," and he quietly left the room, shutting the door behind him, before Hazzard could think of a reply.

What was wrong with the Frenchman? Everyone seemed suspicious of everyone else. Was this one of the reactions that came from the knowledge there was a spy in their midst?

*   *   *

9.
WHO'S GEORGE?

*T*hat night Hazzard was brought face to face with the animosity that existed between the German and the Frenchman. As Chang had said, it was still the French underground against the Nazi.

Hazzard had been called to supper by Wong, who did not speak, but made motions of eating with his hands and pointed to the large room of the quarters. Only Stürmer and Maurice were present. Doctor Kelly was still busy in the hospital with his newly arrived penicillin.

The Frenchman and the German sat at opposite ends of the table and remained silent throughout the meal. As Wong cleared his place, Hazzard decided to try some friendly conversation in an effort to break through the hostile atmosphere.

"Well, at least it's quiet around here," he ventured.

Stürmer turned his head slowly toward Hazzard and spoke without expression. "What is there to talk about?"

Stürmer's attitude riled Hazzard, and he leered back at the German. "The weather," he said sarcastically.

"It is always the same here," said Stürmer, and before Hazzard could reply to this, the German looked away as though he considered the conversation at an end.

Stürmer was now staring at the hunched form of Maurice, who was bent over the table intent on finishing the last of his meal. With a trace of a cynical smile touching the corners of his mouth, Stürmer rose and walked slowly toward the old upright piano across the room.

Maurice, who had been just about to take a drink from his metal cup, paused as though he sensed something was not quite right, and followed the movements of Stürmer with a look of hatred and suspicion.

Stürmer had seated himself at the piano and was running his fingers carelessly across the keys. Hazzard's eyes went from Stürmer to Maurice and back. He did not know what was wrong, but Hazzard could feel the tension building up in the room and he knew something was about to happen. Something that had the smell of death and hatred.

Stürmer stretched his fingers out above the keyboard and began to pick out the notes of Lili Marlene with his right hand.

The tin cup hit the table with a crash, startling Hazzard. The Frenchman had risen to his feet, his faced puffed and red, and corded muscles were standing out on his bull-like neck.

"Do not play that!" he growled but Stürmer continued to play as though the words had not been spoken.

Hazzard saw the Frenchman's mouth begin to quiver with rage and suddenly Maurice was at the piano, pounding on the keys.

"Do not play that song, I say!" he ranted in a thundering voice. "Do not play that song! Do not play! Do not play!" he repeated over and over, his hands keeping time with the words as he brought them crashing down upon the keys of the piano.

Stürmer had stopped playing, and was now looking up at the red and sweating face of Maurice with the look of a man who has just tied a tin can to the tail of a dumbfounded dog. Then, calmly, he turned back to the piano and began once more to pick out the melody of Lili Marlene.

Maurice stood behind the German, clenching and unclenching his ham-like fists in frustration. The blood was pounding in his head and pulsing visibly through the veins on his neck and temples. It was the moment of no return, and Hazzard braced himself to spring up and separate the two men from the death struggle that seem inevitable.

The melody went on and on, becoming louder and louder as each time Stürmer bore down harder on the keys. Maurice turned and walked stiffly to the makeshift bookcase. He pawed through the old newspapers and magazines, picked up a phonograph record, and put it on the turntable of the ancient hand-wind machine. Soon, through the crackle and clicks of a much used record, came the loud sounds of a military band playing La Marseillaise.

At the first sounds of the record, Stürmer stopped playing. Maurice grinned and called across the room. "You give up, oui?"

Stürmer remained motionless at the piano, listening to the record. Then, coming to a decision, he rose and walked toward Maurice.

Here it comes, thought Hazzard, and braced himself again.

The Frenchman's eyes lit up with anticipation of the fight he knew was coming, then, just as quickly, changed to a look of confusion. Stürmer had walked past him, and now stood gazing down at the scratchy record. Slowly Stürmer reached down, carefully lifted the needle arm, and shut off the spring motor of the turntable. Maurice gasped, his face a mixture of surprise and disbelief.

Stürmer was now walking across the room, erect and proud, and whistling loud and airily the strains of Deutschland Über Alles.

Hazzard watched the German stride from the room and out into the night. A sigh escaped from his tensed lungs as the danger of a clash between the two dissolved—but he had relaxed too soon.

The sharp notes of the German anthem had fallen like fuel on the smouldering, maniacal rage of Maurice, and now, the sudden

banging of the bamboo door as it slammed behind the departing
Stürmer became the trigger that set off the explosion in the
Frenchman's brain. Cursing God and the devil in French, Maurice
plunged across the room, tore a machete from the wall, and crashed
out through the door before Hazzard realized what was happening.

Hazzard leaped from his chair, dashed to the door, and just as
quickly stopped. He backed up quietly, swung around, and walked
back to his chair, a relieved smile on his face. One glance had been
enough to make him realize these episodes must be routine by
now. The very fact both the Frenchman and the German were still
alive should have been proof there was something to prevent them
from killing each other.

Maurice had been standing on the wide veranda, and Moro,
Stürmer's ever present shadow, had been standing on the ground
in front of the Frenchman, a cold look in his emotionless eyes, and
a long, slender dagger held loosely in his hand.

Hazzard sat and settled back in his chair to wait. This place
was becoming more interesting by the minute, and now he wanted
to see what would happen next. He knew Moro would not kill
Maurice, and he also knew the Frenchman would not stand outside on the veranda all night long. He wondered if the next scene
in this ridiculous drama would be as amazing as the last.

The hollow sound of footsteps on the warped boards of the
veranda brought his gaze back to the door as Maurice stepped into
the room. The Frenchman was staring beady eyed at the now useless machete in his hand, and whirling around, he stuck it deep
into the rough log door jamb.

Hazzard watched the big man slump down exhausted in a
chair and wondered how soon the day would come when Moro
would not be quick enough to stop them from tearing each other
to bits.

"Those two been at it again?" said the voice of Kelly, and
Hazzard turned to see the doctor standing in the doorway.

Kelly pulled the machete from the wood and looked at the

now limp form of Maurice. "Looks like the French lost the last battle," he remarked.

"Someday I will crush him with my bare hands," retorted Maurice. Then, he jerked his head up and stared angrily at Kelly. "And you, monsieur le docteur, you with the always talking mouth, why you no go someplace else with your little bottle, eh? Crawl in a hole, or maybe jump in the ocean, eh?"

Doctor Kelly placed the machete on the table and shook his head in mock concern. "Temper is very bad for the blood pressure. Especially a big man like you." He winked at Hazzard. "But right now it's time for our favorite radio program. We call him Hanoi Harry."

This last was all a mystery to Hazzard, but any questions he had were drowned out by the loud rush of static as Doctor Kelly switched on the battered military receiver that stood on top of the piano. He turned the dial until the room was filled with the weird squeals of Chinese music, then picking up a bottle and three glasses from the bookcase, he came and sat beside Hazzard at the table.

Kelly poured out three healthy portions in the glasses and pushed one toward Hazzard.

"Thanks," said Hazzard as he accepted the glass. "This is just what I need."

Maurice came to the table without a word, grabbed a glass and returned to his chair. The music from the radio stopped and a voice began to speak in Vietnamese.

Hazzard was about to speak but the doctor held up his hand and shook his head. Then the voice on the radio changed to English.

"This is Radio Hanoi, the voice of the people, with five minutes of today's news in English. But before giving you the news, we would like to take this time to welcome a newly arrived visitor to our country, Mister Michael Hazzard."

Hazzard sat bolt upright in his chair and stared at the radio, but the announcement seemed to have no effect on either Maurice or the doctor, and the voice droned on.

"We hope you will find your stay at Tu-Hao-Tuc an enjoyable one, but being a stranger here, we feel it is our duty to warn you. The jungle can be very dangerous, especially at night."

The voice paused, and the doctor smiled at the surprised expression on Hazzard's face.

"And now for tonight's news. In the United States today, the president issued another of his aggressive, imperialistic notes to the world . . ."

The doctor went over and switched off the radio. He came back to the table and filled his glass again. "Well," he said to Hazzard. "You've made the honor list, and on the first day, too. George was really on the ball today."

"George?" said Hazzard. "Who's George?"

Kelly poured the raw whisky down his throat and let a stream of air gush out between his teeth. "Didn't Chang tell you about George? Well, George is the name we gave to the unknown double-dealer in our midst who keeps informing on us."

"Informing on you?" said Hazzard, knowing it was better to feign ignorance, since any knowledge of the spy could compromise the job he had agreed to do for Chang.

"Yes, informing," continued Kelly. "We have many different types of human derelicts here as you can see, and one of them is a spy."

Maurice came to the table and poured more whisky in his glass. "It is nothing to worry about, Monsieur Hazzard. Everyone us has heard his name on that radio before." He gulped down the drink and shrugged his shoulders. "Anything you do in the day," he pointed at the radio. "He knows about it at the night. But the radio means nothing."

He set the empty glass down, and bending over with both hands on the table, he looked directly into Hazzard's eyes. "Monsieur Hazzard," he said in a low voice, "The question is—who is this spy?"

Yes, thought Hazzard, and maybe the spy was here in the room with him right at this moment . . .

*   *   *

10.

TO SLEEP LIKE A CORPSE

*H*azzard lay awake for a long time. It was not the heavy heat under the mosquito netting, or the night noises of the jungle that kept him from sleeping. He was physically tired, but his mind was racing with too many thoughts, like jigsaw pieces that have become mixed up with the wrong puzzle.

He thought over everything that had happened to him since the night he had been worked over in the alley near his office. Things had certainly gone fast. So fast, he was still confused about what actually had happened to bring him thousands of miles to lie sweating under a mosquito net in the heat of a tropical jungle infested with hatred and war.

Catch the spy. It was not like looking for a needle in haystack; it was more like looking for a needle in a stack of needles. They all looked alike, but which one was the right needle? Since everyone was under suspicion, he had met quite a few suspects since he had arrived.

First we eliminate Ling Ling. For the time being. She had nothing to gain; everything to lose by being the informer. Next, we eliminate yours truly, Michael Hazzard.

Chang? Set him aside for a little while. Calling Hazzard in to help would be a perfect cover to divert suspicion.

Ming Lee? First, we find out if he could have a possible motive to turn traitor. Then, find out if he really doesn't know any English. Set him aside on the same shelf with Chang for a while.

Maurice? Wife and son killed by the commies. Or were they? This would have to be proven. Was Chang's information about the Frenchman based on fact or hearsay? Then, there was the vendetta with the German. It looked real enough, but could be an act.

Stürmer? Once a Nazi. A Nazi was supposed to hate communists. Had Stürmer ever been a prisoner of the Russians and possibly been brainwashed over to their side?

Moro? He was either what he appeared; a watch dog with blind loyalty, or, if Stürmer was a Red agent, there was the possibility of Moro being in on the deal.

Hold up now, Hazzard old boy. Chang had said spy, why not spies? It would be easy for two to operate, one diverting suspicion from the other. This did not have to be Stürmer and Moro. It could be any two in the whole area. This was something to keep in mind.

Who else? Doctor Kelly? Entirely different from the others. Drinks to excess. One of the big Don'ts in the spy manual. Talks too much and plays the philosopher. This could be an act, but the drinking was for real.

A short list of names for the first day, and tomorrow would see other names added to the list. How many people at Tu-Hao-Tuc? A thousand or more? Would each have to be checked out?

How did the spy operate? He had to have a radio, or access to one. The news of Hazzard's arrival had spread to Hanoi too fast for any other method. It could not have come from the Queen Wilhelmina, or from the group of men who had taken him from the ship. None of these people had known the reason for his coming. Everyone, including himself, had thought he was being kidnapped to be held as a hostage. So we come back to the radio. There was no other way. This meant there would be evidence in or close to the village. There would be the radio itself. It might be small and portable, easily concealed anywhere in the jungle. Then there was the possibility of code books. Would these be left in the jungle? No, thought Hazzard, if someone discovered the radio and code books together, the spy would be out of business. Discovery of just the radio would only make operations difficult for a time. Where would you keep a code book? Hazzard remembered the old story of The Purloined Letter. It had been in an obvious place, where all the letters were kept, and proved to be the best hiding place—right in front of your eyes.

From tomorrow, he would start methodically looking through the magazines and papers in the living room of the quarters. You have to start someplace, and if you drew a dud, you moved on.

He had been thinking with his eyes shut, and now he felt a quiver in the short hairs on the back of his neck. He opened his eyes and remained still. Someone was in the room. He could not see or hear anything, but he knew he was not alone. This warning had never failed him before. He focused his eyes on the door and saw nothing but an oblong of black. It was open. He lay tensed and waiting.

A silent shadow floated up from the floor beside his bed, and Hazzard's heart raced as his startled senses reacted to this sudden phantom-like presence. Then he saw the arm being raised, the blade of a long, slender dagger held firmly in a hand, and he lunged sideways to the floor between the mosquito netting and the bed. Once free of the netting, he rolled away from the bed and struck out at the legs he knew would be there. But there was nothing. He continued the roll and came up on his feet in a crouched position. Someone was running down the hallway. Hazzard leaped through the open door just in time to hear the rear door bang shut. Throwing caution to the wind, he tore down the hall and exploded out of the door into the night.

The air was cool and nothing stirred. Hazzard did not know which way his assailant had gone. He turned around the corner of the building to come face to face with Moro. The small Oriental just stood and looked at Hazzard. If the attacker had come this way, Moro would have seen him, unless the attacker was Moro. Hazzard realized that questioning the man would be useless, he would not understand English, and even if he could communicate with Moro, the answers probably would not be satisfactory.

Hazzard turned around and went back into the building, leaving Moro standing under Stürmer's window.

Hazzard stood in the center of his room, deep in thought. Someone did not like Michael Hazzard. There was only one possible answer. Someone knew the real reason for Hazzard's presence in Tu-Hao-Tuc. Now that he knew his cover had been blown, Hazzard would have to move with extreme caution, and come up with a fast solution to the identity of the spy. Every minute the spy remained at large was another minute Hazzard's life would be in jeopardy. Hazzard did not like the thought of this in the least.

One attempt had failed—so logically, the killer would try again. Leave us not present him with the same opportunity, thought Hazzard.

He grabbed the two blankets from the bed, wrapped them around his body and sat on the floor with his back against the door. Pulling the blankets up over his head and face, he leaned back to listen to the night sounds of the jungle. He had intended to stay alert for the rest of the night, but soon the fatigue and tenseness of the last three days overtook his body and his head drooped forward in sleep.

The blazing morning sun came up out of the ocean and streaked into Hazzard's room, focusing on his face that now lolled uncovered against the door. He squinted as it woke him and looked up at the annoying light coming through the window. It took several minutes for the sleep to clear from his brain and for him to figure out what it was he sensed was wrong.

The sun was streaming in through a large gash in the bamboo shutter. He shook his head. What did it mean? Then he saw it. Extending out from a hole torn in the mosquito netting was the shaft of a long native spear that had passed through the mattress and embedded itself in the wall below the cot.

Hazzard pulled the spear from the bed and stood it in a corner of the room. Persistent devil, he thought. Well, it was about time to get busy doing something, and staying in the room was becoming a bit unhealthy. He dashed some cold water on his face and looked in the mirror. The hell with shaving. If the local girls did not like five o'clock shadow early in the morning, they could all go take a flying leap at the moon.

Outside, in the large room of the quarters, he found Maurice and Stürmer finishing their breakfast of syrupy rice and boiled vegetables. The Frenchman grunted a good morning, and Stürmer only nodded as he began to busy himself with the cleaning of his Luger.

It's still quiet around here, thought Hazzard. Like a silent movie. Lots of action, but no dialogue. He finished the breakfast that Wong brought him with a lukewarm cup of bitter coffee and rose to leave as Doctor Kelly came through the doorway from his room.

"Good morning, Mr. Hazzard," beamed the now sober doctor. "Have a good night's sleep?"

Hazzard paused by the door and swung around to face the three of them.

"Yep," he answered cheerfully. "Slept just like a corpse."

Their reactions were identical. Each looked at Hazzard with a mixed expression of curiosity and wonder. And fuck you, too, thought Hazzard as he walked out into the compound.

A small boy came running up and answered the question that was in Hazzard's mind.

"Misser Chang say come." The boy turned away and Hazzard followed him through the village and into the jungle until they came to a large clearing where Chang was addressing a mangy-looking group of forty guerrillas in French.

When he finished, he turned to Hazzard. "I said you will be in charge of them. I also told them you are a great warrior of many battles, and a great leader of men."

"What did you tell them that for?" said the surprised Hazzard.

"You will have enough trouble with them as it is," Chang told him. "I am only trying to make it easier for you. It is up to you to prove you can lead them."

Hazzard looked at the men who were now his responsibility. They looked as bad, if not worse, than the refugees he had seen, and this bunch seemed to lack any semblance of discipline. They stood in various positions, some leaning on rifles, and some squatting on the ground. Each looked back at him with open, unashamed eyes, a few with amusement, a few with arrogance, but all without fear. Hazzard remembered what a South Korean army officer had once told him: "If you are to lead men into danger, you must gain their respect at the very beginning, and as quickly as possible. The secret is in knowing how to get the respect."

Looking at this tough band of undisciplined guerrillas, Hazzard knew there was only one language they would understand.

"Do you have a training area for hand-to-hand combat?" he asked Chang.

"Yes, we have a large pit of sand on the other side of the village."

"Good," said Hazzard as his eyes searched through the group of men and he mentally made his choice. "I think that's where we shall start our first training lesson."

Chang marched the men to the sand pit as Hazzard tried to memorize the commands that were given in a mixture of French and Vietnamese.

The men were lined up around the pit as Hazzard stepped out onto the sand and walked across to stand in front of the biggest and surliest of the lot. He poked the big man in the chest and motioned him to step into the pit. The man grinned at his comrades and looked at Hazzard with a sneer on his lips as he walked into the center of the arena.

"You savvy English?" asked Hazzard.

"Huh?" came the man's half-hearted, grunted reply.

Hazzard pointed to his mouth. "English," he repeated. "Parley English?"

"No speak," said the big man. Then, encouraged by a wave of laughter from the men, he raised his voice and shouted again, "No speak!" And began to laugh.

"No speak, eh?" said Hazzard. "Well, we'll see how much you're laughing five minutes from now."

Taking the bayonet from its scabbard, Hazzard snapped it on the man's rifle, and stepping back, motioned for the man to come at him with the bayonet. At first the big guerrilla cocked his head, wondering what was expected of him, but as Hazzard continued the motions, the man finally began to understand and a big smile spread across his ugly face. Pointing the rifle at Hazzard, he began a slow, half-hearted charge as though he was playing some sort of game and was reluctantly humoring the childish whims of the stupid foreigner.

The big man lunged, flipped through the air, and landed on his back to stare up at Hazzard, who was now holding the rifle with the bare bayonet held only inches from the man's throat.

There was a burst of laughter from the men as Hazzard motioned the man to get up and try it again. This time, with the embarrassment of the first humiliating defeat screaming for revenge, the big man came charging at Hazzard with murder in his eyes.

The result was the same, but for one slight difference. Because of the speed with which he had attacked, the Oriental had hit the ground twice as hard.

Again Hazzard stood over him holding the rifle, the bayonet pointing agonizingly close to the man's throat.

This time there was no laughter from the men, only low mutterings of amazement as Hazzard gave the man back the rifle and motioned for him to do it again. Two defeats in a row were too much for the haughty temper of the big guerrilla, who prided himself on being the strongest one of his group. He walked to the edge of the pit, handed his rifle to one of the men, and turned to face Hazzard with a dagger in his hand. The rifle with a bayonet was a new weapon to this uneducated Oriental, but he had been raised with a dagger and schooled since childhood in its gory uses. Now, watch the fear show in the eyes of this insolent foreigner.

The foreigner was grinning and beckoning to him. This tall stranger was a fool. He would not kill him. A small slash across the face would mark him forever. That would be enough.

Hazzard crouched and waited. The way the guerrilla advanced told him the man was an expert with the knife, but maybe the big man was too sure of himself. Hazzard would know the answer in the next few seconds.

The man lunged, bringing the knife upwards and across toward the belly. Hazzard sucked in his guts as the blade flashed by. The man continued his forward motion and brought the dagger up in a swinging arc at Hazzard's face. Reaching out, Hazzard grabbed the knife arm by the wrist, threw his back and hip swiftly into the man's middle, and as the guerrilla flipped up and over through the air, he deftly wrenched the knife out of the man's hand.

The group of men broke into a loud roar. Hazzard reached down, hauled the big man to his feet and handed him back the knife. Then as Hazzard slapped him on the shoulder in approval, the dumbfounded expression disappeared from the guerrilla's face and he began to laugh and pound Hazzard on the back.

After that it was simple. The men would do anything Hazzard told them. He had hit at their basic primitive motivation; the survival of the fittest, and by downing the biggest brute among them, he had proven he was the fittest. This came out to the natural conclusion that Hazzard was the undisputed leader.

*   *   *

A month went quickly by, and Hazzard's only accomplishment had been to weld his forty rough charges into a well-trained and fairly disciplined fighting unit, but the real problem; that of the mysterious spy, remained in its original state of stagnation.

Hazzard managed to leaf through every book, magazine and newspaper in the quarters. He thoroughly searched the rooms of Stürmer, Maurice, and Doctor Kelly. Even the radio shack used by Chang for guerrilla activities had not escaped a complete going over. He had found nothing.

Every night, since first hearing his name mentioned by Hanoi Harry, he had listened to Radio Hanoi, but there had been no more notices for anyone at Tu-Hao-Tuc.

Even the would-be killer had not tried again since the morning Hazzard had found the spear imbedded in his cot, and he had not mentioned anything to Chang, or to anyone else, about these two attempts on his life.

To all outward appearances, everything at Tu-Hao-Tuc had returned to normal, but Hazzard instinctively knew the spy had only relaxed his activities until a new attempt to kill Hazzard would be assured of success, or until the time came to forward new information to the Viet Minh in Hanoi.

There was nothing more he could do now but wait for the spy to make a move, and so he occupied himself with the training program he had set up for his men. He might never find the spy, but he was sure of one thing—his men would be able to give a good account of themselves in battle, and he was proud of them. It had not been easy. The language barrier was insurmountable and Hazzard had to improvise a simple language of pantomime mixed with whistling and a few words he had managed to pick up to instruct the men in weapons usage, field tactics, hand-to-hand fighting, and the hundreds of other things necessary for a soldier to stay alive in combat.

He had given them a rough schedule of rifle practice, forced jungle marches, bayonet drill, judo, obstacle courses, machine-gun firing, squad tactics, small arms maintenance, and rough and ready discipline. The men seemed to thrive on it, and in turn taught Hazzard what they knew about the jungle.

It had taken only one month, and now Hazzard found himself secretly wishing for a brush with the Reds. The ultimate test of the fighting man—actual combat.

*   *   *

11.
CAPTAIN CHEN SHU WEN

*T*he intelligence center of the 4th Brigade, Viet Nam Liberation Army at Hanoi was a smoothly run, efficient organization, and Wu Chin Lee wanted to keep it that way.

Wu Chin Lee was a colonel in the Secret Police of the Chinese People's Army, but now he wore the uniform of North Viet Nam. It was this way with all the Chinese volunteers who had been ordered to serve in Viet Nam. Colonel Wu was the commander of intelligence of the 4th Brigade, and his office also controlled the activities of communist agents throughout the Indochina-Malay Peninsula as far south as Singapore. He was originally from North China, tall, thin, lean, with a leathery face composed of high cheekbones, a grim unsmiling mouth, and fierce, deep-set, cruel eyes. His position was a powerful one. Though the ordinary rank and file generals in various arms of service of the Viet Nam Liberation Army did not come under his jurisdiction, Colonel Wu's merest suggestion was always immediately acted upon as though it was a direct order from Ho Chi Minh himself. For was it not so that the slightest unfavorable mention of one's name in Colonel Wu's reports brought instantaneous disciplinary action of the People's Court down upon one's head. This could mean demotion in rank at the very least, or quick dismissal, prison, and sometimes even death by a People's firing squad.

Colonel Wu knew his power, but he also knew the power of the people above him, and to antagonize them with mistakes or inefficiency was to tempt the Gods of fate.

Since the time he had taken over command of the intelligence center in Hanoi, he had been bothered by the continued existence of the guerrilla camp at Tu-Hao-Tuc. He had managed to plant an agent in the midst of these traitors, and because of the spy's excellent reports, they had successfully ambushed each guerrilla raid over the last six months.

A tremendous file had been built up on this one operation. He now had maps of the village, of the seacoast and surrounding jungle area, details of all defensive positions, complete lists of food, ammunition, weapons, medical supplies, and a detailed roster of all personnel, including the stupid foreign devils, who had been hired as mercenaries.

Now, he sat at his desk looking angrily at the thick file before him. There had been no reports from his agent in over a month, and among the dispatches received daily from Giap's headquarters there was always one inquiring about the present situation at Tu-Hao-Tuc that always ended with a demand for an immediate reply.

Colonel Wu pivoted his chair around and looked up at the large map spread across the wall behind his desk. It was covered with various colored pins. He stared at the only red pin on the map. It stuck out prominently from the spot marked Tu-Hao-Tuc, but Colonel Wu felt it was hanging over his head like the sword of Damocles.

When he had received this assignment from Peking, he had hoped it would lead to better things. The operation against the South Vietnamese should have gone smoothly and been over within a matter of months. Then the stupid Americans had entered the picture. They brought endless amounts of food, medical supplies, weapons, and ammunition and gave them freely to the South Vietnamese government. They trained the soldiers in modern jungle tactics, and led them with hardened, well-trained Special Forces Troops. The activities of the Americans provided endless material for the communist propaganda ministry, but it failed to have the desired effect of stopping the Americans.

As if this had not been bad enough, the ignorant peasants had been banded together in various localities by a few skilled organizers to form guerrilla bands behind the lines of the Viet Nam Liberation Army. One by one, these nests of subversion had been liquidated or neutralized. Now, there remained only one of major importance, and Colonel Wu was determined to eliminate it as quickly as possible, especially since he firmly believed his agent had finally been compromised.

He picked up one of the telephones on his desk and sent for Captain Chen Shu Wen. If one wanted something done thoroughly, it is always best to use the most capable man available, and Captain Chen had proved his reliability and resourcefulness many times during the conflict in Korea.

Captain Chen had originally been in command of a small intelligence unit charged with smuggling code books and heroin into South Korea for the use of Red agents. Later, because of his ability with the English language, he had been given command of the Special Interrogation and Information Section for English Speaking Prisoners of War. It was a long and imposing title and boiled down to one thing, changing the political beliefs of English speaking prisoners.

This was later referred to as brain-washing among the capitalistic countries. He had been successful in over fifty cases, and more than one third of them had elected to stay in North Korea or China when the fighting ceased. These men were the infamous turncoats of the Korean War, and Chen was rightly proud of these accomplishments for which he had received his captaincy and the Order of Sun Yat Sen, First Class.

Captain Chen also had the dubious honor, although long forgotten, of having personally interrogated a prisoner by the name
of Michael Hazzard, who had been captured during the last two
months of the war. These meetings with Hazzard were lost in the
jumbled memory of hundreds of American and British faces Captain Chen had seen in the many prisoner of war camps. He would
never know his face was burned indelibly into the memory of one
American POW, who had stood by the bed of a dying nineteen
year old prisoner—dying because he had been put on a water diet
by Chen for refusing to answer questions. An American who had
sworn a terrible oath of revenge. It had been the only time in his
life Michael Hazzard had ever sworn to kill a man, and asked God
to be his witness.

Captain Chen snapped to attention before the squint-eyed
gaze of Colonel Wu. Chen also wore the uniform of the army of
North Viet Nam, and proudly displayed over his left breast pocket
was the red and yellow ribbon of the Order of Sun Yat Sen. Colonel Wu looked at the short, fat form of Captain Chen, and the
greasy, bloated face from which two puffy eyes appeared to be on
the verge of being popped out by the surrounding layers of oily
blubber. Chen's usual haughty and arrogant attitude had been left
outside. He was now the essence of military dignity, a soldier re-
porting to his commanding officer, and of all the military commanders in the Southeast Asia District, Colonel Wu was the most
feared—and therefore, the most respected.

Colonel Wu did not return the salute. It was a custom that
disgusted him. "Be seated, Captain Chen," he said. "I have an
interesting problem, which I am going to give to you. I hope very
much you will be able to solve it within the next few weeks. In
fact, I will be more specific. I would be pleased if the problem is
solved in exactly two weeks."

Captain Chen knew from experience this was not a request,
but an order. Then, as was the custom, he accepted the problem
without first finding out what it was.

"I find it a great honor to serve," said Chen. "I pledge my

reputation, and that of my ancestors, to solve the problem before the end of two weeks."

Here is another fool of a conformist, thought Wu. Good. Without them there would be no one to blame for the ever increasing mistakes invariably occurring in a communist-run state.

"You are, of course, familiar with the band of terrorists who inhabit the village of Tu-Hao-Tuc," and the Colonel waited for the assenting nod from the Captain before continuing. "Our agent there has not communicated with us in over one month. Because of this we must move quickly to wipe this blemish from our peaceful land."

Captain Chen smiled. "I am happy to hear I shall be given the honor of their destruction. I had previously asked to be allowed to lead a force against these traitors."

"Previously it was not deemed necessary," said the Colonel with a sharp voice. "With continuous reports from our agent, we were able to meet each of their clumsy raiding parties with our superior troops. This kept them in check, and allowed us to deploy our troops more effectively in other areas. Now, we must move quickly before they contemplate some foolish action that will be embarrassing to report to Commander General Vo Nguyen Giap."

"The agent has been captured?"

"He has either been captured, or turned traitor," replied the colonel.

"And if I should find this agent alive at Tu-Hao-Tuc. . . ?"

"He is to be executed along with any other survivors."

Captain Chen smiled and nodded his head in approval.

"Here is the complete file on this operation," and the colonel shoved it across the desk. "It is most complete. I will send out a request today to give you four companies from the 300th Regiment. You may use your own methods in dealing with this problem. Do not return here until you have succeeded. You have two weeks."

The interview was over, and Chen knew he was dismissed.

Without a word he picked up the heavy file, saluted briskly and left the room.

The call from Colonel Wu was put through quickly, and his polite request for four companies was immediately granted by the commander of the 300th Regiment. The commander was relieved that the personal telephone call from Colonel Wu had been nothing more than a request for troops, and he settled down again into his daily routine of relaxing with his fellow officers and their locally procured concubines.

Captain Chen went over his plans with the officers of the four infantry companies. He would use the whole two week period. It is not wise to be hasty, especially when there is fighting to be done in the jungle. It would take two days to gather the necessary supplies and ammunition, six days of forced marching through the jungle, two days to reconnoiter the village, and two days to deploy the troops. They would attack on the thirteenth day, and by the last day of the allotted period the area would be secured.

Three days after the interview with Colonel Wu, Captain Chen and his four companies were deep in the jungle, heading southeast toward the coast and Tu-Hao-Tuc. Chen had also brought twenty of his own special troops with him. He had assigned four men to each company headquarters section on the pretense of guarding the officers, who were grateful for the captain's apparent consideration of their safety. They did not know Chen had given his men special instructions to make absolutely sure all his orders would be obeyed immediately and without question by the company commanders. To refuse would mean their death.

The remaining four men carried a small portable field transmitter-receiver with which Chen could keep in daily contact with the intelligence center at Hanoi.

Everything was under control, his rigid time schedule was being adhered to, and Captain Chen gloried in his importance and efficiency as he followed the beaten trail the lead company had trampled through the underbrush.

He would destroy Tu-Hao-Tuc in such a way as to leave an

example that would live forever in the minds of the rebellious peasants, and at the same time be called to Peking. There would be speeches, possibly a promotion, most surely another decoration. Colonel Wu had chosen wisely. Captain Chen would not forget the colonel who had been the one to send him on to further glory.

*   *   *

12.

THE CODE BOOK

*C*hang had heard rumors of what Hazzard had done with his unruly bunch of backward farm peasants, and had finally decided to go and see for himself. He found Hazzard sitting lazily against a tree watching his men run through the complicated exercises of setting up mortars in firing positions.

"You have even surprised me, Mr. Hazzard," remarked Chang when he saw the precision movements of the men. "The way you have trained these men is remarkable. I still do not see how you managed it in such a short period of time, especially when you do not speak the language."

"I gave up trying to speak to them," said Hazzard. "Here, watch this," and placing two fingers in his mouth, he whistled two short blasts. The men stopped immediately and looked toward Hazzard who was motioning weirdly with his hands. They quickly dismantled the mortars, ran to the other side of the clearing and set them up again.

"We worked out a set of hand signals for almost everything," explained Hazzard. "And it's a lot better than words. I can run them around in the jungle without a sound by just moving my hands and arms. I've spent a long time teaching them to Big Stoop, and I'm even thinking of making him first sergeant of the group."

"Big Stoop?" said Chang with a frown.

Hazzard smiled. "Big Stoop is a great big giant deaf-mute that a man by the name of Milton Caniff created in a comic strip. And I gave the name to that great big clown who tried to run me through with a dagger the first day in the sand pit. I don't know his real name, and he might as well be a deaf-mute because I can't talk to him anyway. I found out the men will do almost anything he says, so I go over everything in sign language with him first, and then let him do the coaching and set the example. Works out real fine."

"Remarkable," commented Chang.

"Don't get any ideas about making this a permanent job," Hazzard put in quickly. "I'm supposed to be a detective, not a soldier. Remember?"

Chang only nodded his answer and continued to watch the movements of the men. "It is too bad you cannot speak Vietnamese like Doctor Kelly. It would make the training much easier for you."

Hazzard's brain clicked. "Doctor Kelly speaks Vietnamese?"

"I thought you knew. He has lived in Viet Nam for years."

"You never did tell me about Kelly. How long have you known him?"

"He came here about a year ago. Just walked out of the jungle one day. We needed a doctor, so he stayed."

A picture flashed by in Hazzard's mind. It was a picture of a room crowded with bottles, medical instruments, and books. Hundreds of books. How much training do you need before you begin to see the obvious? Kelly's office would be the perfect place. You could hide almost anything in there by just tossing it among the piles of medical rubble.

"Chang, can you get me a flashlight?" asked Hazzard.

"Yes. When do you want it?"

"Right now. I'm going visiting tonight."

*   *   *

The evening meal had been devoured by the four hungry men in the usual friendly atmosphere of complete silence, after which, each had taken up his usual off duty relaxation.

Hazzard sat leafing through an ancient copy of the National Geographic.

Maurice was throwing darts at the two bosomy targets on the nude theater poster, and periodically winding and changing the much used records on the phonograph.

Stürmer sat at the table with an untouched glass of whisky, playing a European variety of solitaire.

Kelly, who had already soaked up half a bottle of whisky, was sprawled out on a chair in a drunken stupor. His right hand clutched a partially filled glass as it dangled over the side of the chair with the bottle cradled in his lap.

Hazzard shifted his eyes from one to the other and pressed his forearm against his leg to feel the presence of the flashlight Chang had given him. He rose, threw the magazine into the chair, and stretched lazily. Turning, he walked leisurely toward the door. Behind him were only the sounds of the darts hitting the wall, and the occasional snap of a card as Stürmer methodically went through the deck. As he reached the door, Kelly's glass hit the floor. The sound seemed twice as loud as it should have been. Hazzard stopped and looked back over his shoulder. Neither Maurice or Stürmer had paid any attention to the noise, and Kelly was too far gone to have noticed an artillery barrage.

Continuing out to the veranda, Hazzard paused to light a cigarette and let his eyes grow accustomed to the darkness. He waited until the cigarette was half gone. Then, glancing back into the room to make sure everyone was still preoccupied with their own amusement, he snubbed the tobacco out, and walked off through the edge of the darkened compound.

Kelly's office in the hospital had somehow escaped Hazzard's notice. He had searched every place there had been books, paper, or writing materials. Lying awake nights, he had wracked his brains to think of a place he could possibly have missed. This was the last place you could possibly hide a code book.

Kelly spoke Vietnamese, and if you were communicating with the commies in this country, you would certainly have to speak the language.

The bamboo-shuttered windows of the hospital glowed with the dim yellow light of candles, but the office was in darkness. Hoping no one would have a reason to come in during the doctor's absence, Hazzard slipped silently up through the heavy shadows and opened the rear door.

Inside, he moved quickly to a row of bookcases he had remembered from his first visit. From here he would work methodically around the room.

After Chang had given him the flashlight, Hazzard had taped tissue paper over the lens to avoid the harshness of the beam of light. Now, he turned it on and it glowed with enough soft light to see in a close area, but not enough to be detected from the outside.

He had worked halfway around the room when a soft noise made him turn off the light and stoop swiftly to the floor. Then he heard a chain rattle against wood, and remembered the mangy monkey the doctor kept in his office. Clucking his tongue against the roof of his mouth brought an answering movement and another rattle of the chain. He turned the light on, cupped the lens in his hand, and saw the two shiny staring eyes of the monkey looking at him from the window sill. Hazzard grinned to himself and went back to his search.

A bamboo shutter rattled slightly. Hazzard heard the noise and passed it off as the movements of the monkey. He did not see the fingers holding the slats of the bamboo apart, or the two eyes watching his movements around the room from outside the window.

Then Hazzard found what he was looking for. It lay beneath a pile of moldy, unused books on a dusty shelf. It was a Chinese telegraph code book. The type used throughout China to send ordinary telegrams.

The Chinese language is made up of thousands of ideographs. Devising a morse-type code for each of these characters would be an impossible task. To be able to send domestic telegrams throughout the country a simple system of numbering was decided upon. The most commonly used characters were arranged in a book. Each page had 100 squares divided into 10 horizontal rows and 10 vertical rows. The characters on each page were all given the same numbers starting with 01 on the upper left, and continuing across each row and ending with the one hundredth square being number 00.

The page number was used for the first two digits of the code group with the second two numbers representing the character on the page. Telegraph code group 2315 would then be character 15 on page 23. A hundred pages would give them a vocabulary of 10,000 characters. Enough for domestic telegraph use.

To send secret messages it would only be necessary to change the numbers of the pages, and for military use, they could rearrange the characters on the pages to suit themselves. Combinations would be almost endless.

Hazzard looked closely at the pages. None of the numbers had been changed, and there was no writing or handwritten notes on any of the pages. The book was exactly like any other telegraph book used throughout the Chinese-speaking world. This meant there would be a slip of paper somewhere, probably carried continuously by the spy, that would indicate the changes needed to actually encode a message.

He put the book back beneath the pile of rubble on the shelf, switched off the flashlight, and quietly left the room.

Cutting back toward the quarters through a small patch of jungle, Hazzard failed to see the silent shadow keeping pace behind him, and then pass around him through the trees like a phantom.

The moon had come up and now it shone brilliantly through

the leaves to make flickering patches of light along the narrow trail. Hazzard had just passed a large vine-covered tree when his foot slipped under a root that bowed up at the edge of the path. He almost fell as the root held firmly across his instep. Bending down to pull it away, he heard the swishing sound of a thrown dagger, and the dull impact as the blade struck solid wood.

There was no sound from the jungle as Hazzard remained bent over and motionless. Reaching inside his shirt, he pulled Sam from his waistband. Then, making sure he would not expose himself in a patch of moonlight, he slowly stood. A shadow flicked among the trees and came closer. Hazzard pulled himself deeper into the shadows and waited. The dim form of a man stood three yards away from Hazzard, and appeared to be intently searching the path.

"Don't move," said Hazzard.

The shadowy form dropped to the ground and dissolved into the darkness of the jungle. Hazzard moved slowly forward. There was no sound, and he knew his stalker was now gone. He pulled the knife from the tree, circled around through the thick under-growth, and returned to the quarters by a different route.

Hazzard was surprised to see Stürmer walking up the steps of the veranda lighting a cigarette. A sound behind him made the already nerve-taut Hazzard spin around to see Moro coming through the trees from the direction of the hospital.

"You have been taking a walk?" said the voice of the German.

Hazzard looked at Stürmer, and then back at the approaching Moro. "Yeah, a walk," replied Hazzard as he moved up the steps past Stürmer and through the door.

Kelly was alone in the room standing by the phonograph, and apparently as sober as a judge. He looked up from the record he was holding as Hazzard entered. "You shouldn't go walking in the jungle alone at night," he said.

"How do you know I was in the jungle?" asked the suspicious Hazzard.

"Look at your boots," said Kelly.

Hazzard glanced down and saw a sprig of leaves entangled in the laces.

The rear door slammed, then following the sound of heavy footsteps, Maurice came into the room and stopped at the sight of the dagger in Hazzard's hand.

Stürmer, Moro, and Maurice had all been outside. Any one of them could have been the knife thrower. Hazzard thought of the leaves in his boot laces as he glanced at Kelly's feet. They were clean, but his trousers were stained at the knees. Were these fresh stains, or had they been there before? Hazzard could not remember, but it meant Kelly could also have been in the jungle at the same time.

Hazzard turned around. They were all staring at him. Stürmer from the doorway. Moro from the veranda. Maurice and Kelly from their position by the phonograph. Each looking at the dagger that Hazzard held in his hand.

The corner of his eye caught the life-size theater poster, and flicking his arm upward and sideways, he threw the knife at the image of the nude stripper. It thudded into her midsection just above the belly button.

There was no reaction from among his impromptu audience, and swinging around to go to his room, Hazzard almost trampled over the grinning houseboy, who jumped quickly to one side to let him pass.

Nothing seemed to happen for a long time. When it did happen, everybody seemed to get into the act.

Someone knew why he was here. They had attempted to kill him twice the first night. Then for a month the spy had ceased all activities and let Hazzard go about his business. He had searched the entire quarters and nothing had happened. He had gone through everyone's room and still nothing had happened. Now, as soon as he had discovered the Chinese telegraph code book, this same someone had known it, and again had tried to kill him.

Was it only a coincidence that Stürmer, Moro, Maurice, and possibly Kelly, had been out at the same time? Could Kelly work in his office everyday for a year and not have seen the telegraph book? It would not be logical for Kelly to hide it there if he were the spy . . . or would it?

All this was getting Hazzard nowhere in a hurry, and he made his mind up to tell Chang everything that had happened since he had arrived at Tu-Hao-Tuc.

*   *   *

13.

THE PLAN

*C*hang and Ling Ling Yung sat impassively in the main room of the villa as they listened to Hazzard.

"And that's the whole story. I have a lot of suspicions. In fact, there are too many suspects, but I haven't found anything except the location of that Chinese telegraph book. To be honest about it, that book might not have anything to do with it. But your spy, whoever he is, knows why I'm here. It makes finding him all the more difficult. He can watch me, but I can't watch him," concluded Hazzard.

Chang remained silent and unmoving for a long time. "Well, I am afraid we can wait no longer," he finally said.

"No," Ling Ling said forcibly. "It is too dangerous. Let us wait a little longer."

"We have already waited too long as it is," said Chang.

"What are you talking about?" asked Hazzard. "Wait for what?"

"Most of our weapons, as you know, were captured from the enemy," Chang explained. "The only place we can get ammunition for them is to raid their supply dumps along the coast. If we should be attacked suddenly, we could fight for only a few hours before our supplies would be exhausted."

"And now you want to go out and raid a few supply dumps?" said Hazzard.

"Yes," replied Chang. "It is the only way. The spy in our midst also knows about our supplies. If the raid should fail, we will lose but a few men, but if we are attacked in force in our present circumstances, we lose everything."

"No matter what you decide, it will be suicide," said Ling Ling.

"This time we will try and be more careful," Chang told her. "Maybe we can keep the traitor from discovering our plans until it is too late. We shall not brief the men until the last moment. Now, I must send for Mr. Paquet, Herr Stürmer, and Doctor Kelly, and outline the plan."

"Wait a minute," broke in Hazzard. "They don't all have to know about this. Why bring them all here?"

"It is the only way," Chang told him. "It is Herr Stürmer's turn to lead the raid, and calling him here alone would give away the fact we were planning something. Calling everyone is not unusual, as we often have meetings here."

"And if one of them is the spy?" said Hazzard.

"That is the chance we will have to take," said Chang as he stood and left the room.

Hazzard sat back in his chair and stared gloomily out across the rocky seacoast as he waited for Chang to return with the others.

"You are not happy here?" said the throaty voice of Ling Ling.

"I am not happy with the way things are going," he told her.

Ling Ling came and sat in the chair beside him, and he shrank from the warm touch of her hand on his arm.

"You are afraid of me?" she said.

Hazzard shot a glance at the ever watching Ming Lee. "I just don't want King Kong there to get any peculiar ideas."

Ling Ling spoke quickly to Ming Lee in Chinese. The giant glared at Hazzard and then left the room.

"Now, we are alone," and she put her hand on his arm again.

He looked across the short distance between them and saw the searching look in her eyes.

"I have not seen you since you first arrived," she said. "It has been a long time."

"Only one month," he told her.

"It seems longer. The time goes so slowly here for me. It is very boring to live in this big house alone. Tell me, what do you do every day?"

As she talked, she kept leaning closer. Too close. Hazzard stood and moved away. A man can take just so much of a woman like this, then his will power will break down with an overpowering urge to take the forbidden fruit.

He turned his back to her and spoke as he looked out across the village. "I get up early every morning, and all day long I train your men to be soldiers. It is very interesting."

"What do you do in the evenings?" she asked.

"I read."

"What do you read?"

"Old magazines."

She had come to his side and was now looking up at his profile. Hazzard did not know whether he wanted to look down into her upturned face or not. She was a temptation Hazzard could not resist for very long, and for some unexplained reason he felt he should not tamper with the feelings of this woman. Maybe it was the thought of the giant Ming Lee, or maybe it was fear. The fear of becoming emotionally involved.

Her voice came in a husky whisper. "I do not think reading old magazines is very interesting. You must find the evenings here as boring as I do."

He looked down at her, and suddenly she was in his arms, her body arching slightly into his. Her lips held firm against the pressure of the kiss. Then, slowly, as the tenseness in her body relaxed, her mouth opened to his, and they devoured each other in a long wanton kiss of passion.

She broke away with a gasp and faced the window, her shoulders trembling under Hazzard's hands.

"You are the first one who has ever kissed me," she said in a low whisper. "You are the first one I have ever wanted to kiss." She turned around to face him. "Is it wrong?"

"To kiss?"

"No. To want a man?"

Hazzard took her chin between his hands and looked down at the unbelievable beauty of the face that had sent this urgency of passion coursing through his veins. "No," he said softly. "It is not wrong."

"Will you come here to see me again?"

"Do you want me to come?"

"Someday you must leave here," she told him. "I want always to carry the memory of you in my heart. Yes, I want you to come."

Hazzard left her question unanswered. He had heard the voices in the corridor and dropped his hands from her face. When the others entered, Ling Ling was standing by the glass-paneled doors gazing out across the sea, and Hazzard sat once more in the chair, his feelings a mixture of emotions he could not understand.

Chang unrolled a detailed chart of the North Vietnamese coastal area on the table before them. Each communist supply dump was clearly marked in red ink with notations of what the dump contained. Hazzard ran his eyes over the chart, scanning the clearly inked English words: small arms depot, 105mm art. shells, clothing, medicine, vehicle tires, mil. rations, etc. There was everything you could possibly need, and the majority of the supply dumps were located along the coast.

Chang gave them a basic outline of the raid. Stürmer would leave the next day and attack a small arms ammunition depot situated in the lightly guarded village of Thai-Binh, located at the head of a narrow bay sixty miles north of Tu-Hao-Tuc. Then, for two hours, they worked out the details; haggling, suggesting, rejecting, and agreeing, until all of them were satisfied.

Stürmer would take forty men with him. They would go up

the coast in two of the armored motorized sampans, regulating their speed so they could enter the bay at eleven fifteen at night, and land at eleven thirty. The population would run into the jungle or remain hidden in their huts at the first sound of gunfire, and the small garrison guarding the warehouses would be quickly dealt with.

The sampans would be loaded with as many cases of small arms ammunition as they could carry and return over the same route. For maximum security, the forty men Stürmer would take with him would not be briefed on the raid until one hour before departure. This way, they hoped, the information could not be transmitted to the Reds by the unknown spy in time for the communists to send reinforcements and ambush the raiding party.

They went over the details of the plan a second time. At each point Stürmer nodded his head in agreement. He had gone on many raids in the past, and this one seemed much simpler than any of the others.

"And you should return here no later than two hours after dawn," concluded Chang. "Do you understand everything?"

"Ja, I understand," said Stürmer.

"And just in case something should go wrong, keep someone listening on your radio constantly until at least eleven ten. After that, it will not make much difference one way or the other."

"I don't see why I can't go," broke in Hazzard. "I haven't done anything but sit around looking at the scenery, and I want a chance to give those roughnecks of mine a little action."

Ling Ling felt a jolt of fear stab at her heart when she heard these words. It had not dawned on her until now that Hazzard would possibly be sent on one of these missions, and the memory of what had happened to all the other raiding parties during the last six months made her shudder as she unconsciously bit her lower lip.

"It is my turn to go," said Stürmer. "Do not worry, Herr Hazzard. Your time will come. All too soon I am afraid."

"Then it is settled," said Chang. "Unless there are any questions."

He looked from one to the other. There were no questions. They all seemed absorbed in their own thoughts, and Hazzard caught himself wondering if one of them was thinking of a Chinese telegraph book and a radio message. Then, abruptly, Kelly stood up.

"Well, if you will all excuse me. I must return to my hospital," he said. "It is time for my evening tonic."

Hazzard watched him leave with growing suspicion. If Kelly was the spy and sent a message to Hanoi now, would the Reds have time to set up an ambush? Then he brushed the thought from his mind.

"Where does the doctor get all his liquor?" he asked. "Way out here at the end of the world?"

"The natives make it," Maurice told him with a laugh. "And Monsieur Kelly thinks the taste will change if he puts it in those fancy bottles."

The door behind Hazzard opened and he turned around to see Wong coming in with a large tray of tea and cups.

"Well, if it's a choice between native moonshine and tea, I guess I'd better stick to tea," and reaching for a cup, he held it up in a toast. "Bottoms up!"

"I wish I had your sense of humor, Herr Hazzard," said Stürmer. "But somewhere, many years ago, I seemed to have lost the virtue of seeing pleasure in anything." He noticed the rest of them were looking at him strangely, and he forced a smile as he took a cup of tea. "But come, let us not be sad."

"Wait!" said the voice of Ling Ling.

The sudden outburst surprised them and they watched her questioningly as she went to a large cabinet and brought a bottle back to the table.

"I have been saving this for some great occasion," she explained. "And I think tonight is as good a time as any to open it."

Maurice gently picked up the bottle. "French cognac," he said reverently. Then he held it up for all to see and laughingly said, "Ah, Monsieur le docteur will kill himself tomorrow when he hears about this."

Ling Ling brought crystal glasses to the table and nodded to Maurice, who opened the bottle and poured the drinks.

"To Herr Stürmer," said Ling Ling as she raised her glass. "May the gods of good fortune go with you."

"No, wait," said Stürmer and he held up his hand. "Do not drink to me. Rather, let us drink to why we are gathered here." He raised his glass. "To freedom and liberty."

These words, coming from Stürmer, stunned everyone into silence and immobility. From another person, at another time, in another place, they would have been laughed off as corny dramatics, but now, especially coming from the usually silent German, they took on a deep meaning of sincerity.

Slowing rising from his chair, and raising his glass, Maurice broke the silence.

"To freedom, liberty . . . and to you, Monsieur Stürmer."

*   *   *

14.
THE RAID

*C*olonel Wu had been awakened in the early hours of the morning by an urgent call from his office at the intelligence center, and now he sat at his desk reading the decoded message from his agent at Tu-Hao-Tuc. He had left standing orders to be summoned immediately if any messages were received from this particular agent.

Now, this nest of troublemakers was planning a raid on the ammunition dump at Thai-Binh. Colonel Wu had less than twenty-four hours to try and stop it. He knew the remoteness of the area and the military situation along that section of the coast would prevent him from sending in any troops before the scheduled time of the raid. There were no naval units close enough to use effectively, and air lifting troops was out of the question.

He picked up the telephone. "I want to know the exact position of Captain Chen and his troops immediately," he snapped, and turned around to study the large map on the wall.

The door opened and a junior officer came in with a file folder and a detailed map of the area north of Tu-Hao-Tuc. Captain Chen's route from Hanoi had been carefully marked on the map, and he was now about twenty miles northwest of Thai-Binh. Twenty miles through the jungle in time to meet the raiders would mean a continuous forced march.

Colonel Wu looked at his watch. It was now ten minutes to four. If a message was sent now, Captain Chen could be on the move by four thirty. This would give him exactly nineteen hours. They would have to travel through dense jungle at over one mile an hour without rest, and be ready for combat when they arrived at Thai-Binh. Under normal conditions this would be impossible for fully equipped troops.

Colonel Wu bent over the map again. There was a dirt road winding down through the jungle from north to south connecting the scattered villages along the coast. Captain Chen was now eight miles southwest of the road at its closest point. If he reached the road at this spot he would have to travel another nineteen miles southeast to reach Thai-Binh. This increased the total distance to twenty-seven miles, but traveling along the road would increase his speed. It was this, or nothing, and the raiding party must be stopped.

"You will transmit this message to Captain Chen at once," he said to the junior officer, and Colonel Wu wrote out the instructions that would send Captain Chen and his four infantry companies to Thai-Binh.

*   *   *

Stürmer's men had been briefed on the coming raid and were now boarding the two armored sampans. Hazzard, Maurice and Chang stood on the wharf with Stürmer, watching the preparations.

The sun had disappeared below the level of the treetops and the short tropical twilight was fast darkening into night. Stürmer walked along the edge of the wharf making one last check of the men and equipment, then looking at his watch, he nodded to the others. "It is time to leave," he said, and strode toward the lead sampan.

Moro jumped aboard and held the boat steady against the wharf, waiting for Stürmer to board. The German hesitated, and then coming back toward Hazzard, he took a cord with a key dangling on it from around his neck.

"Herr Hazzard, will you do me a great favor?" he asked.

"If I can," said Hazzard.

Stürmer held out the key. "This is the key to a metal chest in my room. If I should fail to return, I wish you to open it, pour gasoline inside, and burn everything. Without reading or looking at anything. Will you do this for me?"

"But you'll be back . . ."

"I have your word?" and Stürmer held out his hand.

Hazzard took the key. "You have my word," and shook Stürmer's hand.

Stürmer turned and quickly jumped aboard. The two sampans were poled out toward the mouth of the cove, the motors coughed, then caught, and soon they were lost in the growing dusk. The soft sound of their muffled engines fading away under the noise of the pounding surf.

Kelly was sitting on the steps of the quarters when they returned from the lagoon.

"Has he gone?" he queried.

He received no answer, but he knew by their attitudes the German had left, and he got up to follow them inside.

All of them were apprehensive and nervous. They fidgeted around the room for a long time doing nothing until Chang, in desperation, finally suggested they play poker. They went through the motions of the game automatically, none of them concentrating on the cards or caring whether he won or lost.

*   *   *

When Captain Chen had received the message from Hanoi, he had consulted his map, gotten the men up, and had them moving in fifteen minutes. Ruthlessly he had pushed them through the eight miles of jungle, kicking at those who fell, cursing those who lagged behind, and promising swift punishment to all if they arrived at Thai-Binh too late to stop the raiders. When they had reached the road, he ordered them to alternately run for five minutes and then walk for five minutes. Men fell into the dust of the road under the heavy weight of mortars, shells, and small arms ammunition they carried on their backs, only to be hauled to their feet and shoved harshly along again at the grueling pace.

It had taken nine-and-a-half hours to come the first eight miles, but only six hours to travel the nineteen miles along the road to the village. They had arrived in Thai-Binh at eight ten. Captain Chen let them rest for twenty minutes before ordering the junior officers to deploy two companies on each side of the narrow bay. When this was done, he went in search of the local garrison commander, and demanded to be shown through the warehouse area.

The commander readily agreed, exclaiming his admiration for the past heroic feats of Captain Chen, but in reality, the commander had taken one look at Chen's special papers, and had felt the cold sensation of the icy hand of death on his heart when he saw the imposing seal of the Secret Police of the People's Army.

"What is this building?" asked Chen.

"Small arms ammunition," replied the commander.

"And that building over there?" said Chen, pointing with a bamboo switch.

"A few odd items of communication equipment. Telephone wire, pieces of hardware, a few searchlights, one or two . . ."

"Searchlights?" exclaimed Chen. "Show them to me!"

"But Captain, they are in heavy wooden cases."

"Then open them, stupid!" cried Chen.

The commander ordered his men to break open several cases, revealing a type of small searchlight, about two feet in diameter, that Chen had previously seen attached to poles around various prison camps.

"Do you have generators for these?" he asked.

"We have a few small generators for electricity," replied the weary commander. "But I do not know if they are strong enough for these big lights."

"Commander, you will keep your thoughts to yourself, and confine your talking to direct answers to my questions." Chen paused to allow the effect of this statement to penetrate. "Now, you will bring your generators, these lights, and ten rolls of telephone wire to the places I will show you on this map."

Captain Chen unfolded the map on the top of a crate with the smug satisfaction of one who has just conceived a master plan of strategy, and explained to the commander exactly what must be accomplished before eleven o'clock that night.

*   *   *

"I cannot play this game," muttered Maurice, and he threw his cards into the middle of the table.

"Don't tell me you're worried about Stürmer?" asked the sarcastic Kelly.

"I am not worried about anyone," retorted Maurice. "It is too hot to play with cards." Pushing back his chair, he walked to the life-size nude poster, pulled the darts from the wall, and began throwing them at the naked breasts.

"What time is it?" Chang asked of no one in particular.

"Almost eleven," replied Hazzard.

Chang forced himself to ask the question that had been going through his mind, knowing he must, but not wanting to hear the answer. "What time does the radio usually give those English news broadcasts from Hanoi?"

"At eleven o'clock every night," answered Kelly. "You know as well as I do." He paused a moment. "Do you want to listen?" he asked finally.

"I think I'm afraid to listen, but I cannot change anything by not listening," said Chang. He waved his hand in resignation at Kelly. "Turn on the radio."

Kelly walked slowly to the radio, turned the switch and waited for it to warm up. Static filled the room, and he tuned it until it gave forth the eerie sound of high-pitched Chinese music. Returning to the table, he sat with Chang and Hazzard and absentmindedly began to shuffle the cards. Above the sound of music was the steady thudding of darts as Maurice continued to throw them mechanically at the poster.

Hazzard's watch showed exactly eleven. Any second now, he thought, and as if in answer to his anticipation, the music stopped. A voice spoke in an unrecognizable sing-song language that Hazzard guessed was Vietnamese. There was a long pause, then came the voice of Hanoi Harry.

"This is Radio Hanoi, the voice of the people, bringing you ten minutes of English commentaries on today's world events. But first, a personal greeting to our friends at Tu-Hao-Tuc."

Everyone in the room tensed.

"We send greetings to Doctor John Kelly. You have been at Tu-Hao-Tuc exactly one year today. It is indeed sad such a learned doctor should waste his talents helping the traitors and criminals at Tu-Hao-Tuc. Especially under such poor conditions. How many patients have died this month, doctor? It is a pity you cannot get medicine instead of bullets and guns to cure your patients."

"And now, for a few commentaries on today's events . . ."

"And I hope you die of syphilis, you Red bastard!" commented Kelly.

They all grinned at Kelly's remark. It was as though a heavy weight had been lifted from the room. The atmosphere changed. The tenseness of fearful anticipation was gone. Maurice came back to the table, sat, and grabbed the cards.

"We play the poker. The stud seven card, with the number two card is wild." He looked across at Hazzard to make sure he had correctly learned the American poker jargon, and began to deal.

The voice of Hanoi Harry droned on behind them as he reported the news in English, unheeded by the poker players, who were now concentrating on their cards.

*   *   *

Stürmer stood by the helmsman watching the darker outline of the coast slip by, and occasionally looking behind to make sure the other sampan was maintaining the same speed. It was a clear moonless night, but the stars gave off sufficient light to give them enough visibility to navigate.

Looking at the luminous dial of his watch, Stürmer saw it was almost ten minutes after eleven. Soon they would be turning into the shore and the mouth of the narrow bay. He reached down and tapped the man who sat next to the small battery-operated field radio. The man took off his earphones, turned the radio off, and stood behind Stürmer.

The helmsman snapped his fingers and pointed toward the shore. A black cleft in the dull grayness of the land showed between the steep hills rising on either side of the narrow inlet to Thai-Binh. The two boats turned toward the land, and the engines stopped as Stürmer raised his hand. Two men on the stern of each boat lowered long oar-like sweeps into the water and began to scull the sampans silently through the deepening swells.

*   *   *

Maurice had just bluffed Kelly out of a large pot and was feeling immensely proud of himself when Hanoi Harry came to the end of his nightly propaganda spiel.

"We shall be back tomorrow evening at seven o'clock with five minutes of English news, and again at eleven o'clock with ten minutes of English commentaries on world events. This is Radio Hanoi, the voice of the people . . . I have just received a special bulletin for our friends at Tu-Hao-Tuc . . ."

The effect in the room was electrifying. They all froze, and each could hear his blood pulsating madly in his ears as his heart pounded from the shock of Hanoi Harry's words.

"I have been asked to tell you a wonderful reception party has been arranged at Thai-Binh for Heinrich Stürmer's visit tonight . . ."

Maurice slammed his hands on the table and exhaled a torrent of ugly French.

"You fucking bastards!" yelled Kelly, and threw half the deck of cards at the radio.

"Quick, the radio!" cried Chang, and followed by the others, he dashed through the door, leaving Hanoi Harry monotonously talking to an empty room.

"Radio Hanoi broadcasts daily in the three point five, seven, and fourteen megacycle bands . . ."

When Hazzard arrived at the small radio shack, Chang had already alerted the operator, who was now speaking methodically into a microphone in Vietnamese. Periodically, the operator would stop and listen, but all that came back to them was the rushing hiss of static.

"What time is it now?" asked the anxious Chang.

"Twenty-two minutes after eleven," replied Hazzard.

"He is supposed to land at eleven thirty," said Chang. "We will keep trying."

*   *   *

The two armored sampans had silently entered the narrow bay, and were moving steadily along between the high, steep slopes that bordered the small fishing harbor of Thai-Binh when suddenly they were blinded by the sharp brilliance of searchlights on both sides.

The voice of Captain Chen called out in heavily accented English over a loudspeaker.

"Drop your guns and surrender. There is no escape. If you do not obey at once, you die!"

Stürmer blinked at the lights as a voice repeated the order in Vietnamese. He looked forward to where three men crouched out of sight with a tripod mounted 30-caliber air-cooled machine gun.

"Ready with the machine gun," he called out in a hoarse whisper.

He heard the click of the bolt as they pulled it back to cock and load the weapon.

"Now, fire!" he shouted.

The machine gunners heaved the gun up onto a small deck between the gunwales and began to rake the shore. Instantly both boats erupted with rifle and machine gun fire. A second later, they were met with a withering return fire from both sides of the narrow strip of water.

"Back! Back!" shouted Stürmer. "Start the engines!"

Men standing up to obey were cut down by the intense fire from shore and fell back to the deck that was fast becoming coated with blood.

The radio operator squatted down beside his small set and hurriedly grabbed the earphones. Reaching for the switch, he was driven forward by the impact of machine gun bullets slamming into his back to exit through his chest and continue on to make jagged, bloody holes through the sides of the radio.

Stürmer was firing his Luger ineffectively at the shore. "The lights!" he screamed above the thundering chatter of the guns. "Shoot at the lights! Shoot at the lights!"

He was trying to take careful aim at one of the searchlights when something smashed into his face, and for an instant the scene before him seemed to magnify and dance crazily before his eyes. Then, he was falling into a deep void of soft velvety blackness and silence. He dropped the Luger and started to pitch forward over the rail.

The strong hands of Moro grabbed Stürmer and hauled him back down to the safety of the deck.

"The lights. Shoot the lights," he mumbled as Moro tried to stop the bleeding where the bullet had cut deeply across the eyes and shattered the bridge of Stürmer's nose.

*   *   *

Chang had ordered the radio operator to keep a continuous watch on the frequency the raiding party was using in the false hope they might try to send a message back to Tu-Hao-Tuc. They had then returned to the living quarters to torture themselves by waiting for some kind of news from Stürmer, which they all knew, but would not admit, would never come.

Maurice began again to throw darts, but this time he attacked the poster with a vengeance and growled out oaths in French each time he violently hurled a dart.

Hazzard and Chang had slumped themselves down dejectedly at the table, not knowing what to say or do under the present uncertain circumstances.

Kelly was standing by the bookcase where he kept some of his liquor supply, nervously rattling bottles as he tried to find a full one. Pulling the cork from a bottle that had originally held a fifth of long-forgotten Johnny Walker, he held it to his mouth, letting the raw liquid burn down his throat and spill out over his chin. He gasped, wiped the back of his hand across his mouth, and then wiped his hand on the front of his sweat-stained shirt.

"Did you ever hear this story?" he asked in a loud voice with his back to the room. "Once there were ten little Indians. Ha! Look around you! How many Indians do we have left now?"

"All right, Doctor Kelly," Chang said in a sharp voice. "That will be about enough!"

"What do you mean, enough?" said Kelly, spinning around to face them. "Don't you think we ought to start planning a party? A welcome party for Stürmer's return? A Roman feast for the conquering legion. Hail Caesar! And if things come out for the worse, we can turn it into an Irish wake!"

"You're drunk," said Chang.

"So, I'm drunk. So what? It's a damn sight better than being dead!"

A dart whizzed by Kelly's face and imbedded itself in the wall. Kelly's mouth dropped open as he saw the angry red look on Maurice's face, and he staggered backwards against the bookcase.

"Drink your whisky, you stupid pig," Maurice said through clenched teeth. "Do not talk. Just drink your whisky!" Then, he turned back to the poster to continue his harassment of the nude stripper with his darts.

Kelly mumbled drunkenly to himself as he sat in a large bamboo chair, alternately drinking from the bottle and casting dark glances at the broad shouldered back of the Frenchman.

The night dragged on, and one by one sleep overtook them as they succumbed to the aftereffects of a day of tense nervous strain and excitement.

*   *   *

15.

THE RETURN

*T*he sun rose out of the sea to cast its golden rays along the high cliffs of the rocky coastline. A sleepy guard stood on the edge of a precipice overlooking the ocean and the harbor of Tu-Hao-Tuc, wondering if his relief would be late again this morning as he peered down toward the village. Sometimes he was relieved on time, most often it would be late, and never was it early. Today it would be late. He must remember to be late himself when his turn came again for guard duty. It was a vicious circle of do unto others as they do unto you, and in his simple Oriental peasant mind, it was the only natural and logical thing to do.

He leaned against the uprights holding the alarm bell. It had been retrieved from a temple the Viet Minh had burned to the ground in the early stages of the fighting. Now, it was no longer a voice to summon the gods, but one to summon the quick aid of armed men.

The relief guard was late. He should have come before the sun rose fully out of the sea. Squinting against the horizontal rays beaming across the ocean, he let his eyes rove aimlessly up and down the coast. The morning sun was playing tricks that made him imagine a boat was coming out beyond a spit of land to the north. No, there it was again.

He took a pair of binoculars from a box under the bell. It was a boat. But it was too early for the raiding party to be returning, and besides, the raiders had taken two boats. An attack on Tu-Hao-Tuc by one boat would be stupid, but . . . Putting down the binoculars, he grabbed the heavy, padded hammer, and sent the throbbing peals of the bell echoing down through the jungle.

The village erupted into frenetic activity. Men snatched up weapons and ran to their assigned posts. Women hurriedly grabbed their children and disappeared into safe places of hiding. Ammunition cases were opened, machine guns emplaced, riflemen jumped into camouflaged holes, and through all this, none knew what menace was about to strike.

Chang snapped erect as the sound of the bell penetrated into his sleep filled brain.

"The alarm bell!" he gasped. "It means an attack!"

The door burst open and a breathless soldier rushed in, jabbering in rapid Vietnamese.

"A boat is coming down the coast," Chang told them.

"It might be Stürmer coming back," said Hazzard as he and Maurice followed Chang through the door.

Kelly blinked his whisky red eyes and staggered uncertainly to his feet.

"I gotta see this," he mumbled to himself. "Never saw dead men sail a boat before."

Stopping halfway across the room, he returned to where he had left his half-filled bottle, raised it to his lips and took a long, healthy swig. He set the bottle down on the table. Then, as an afterthought, he picked it up again and walked unsteadily from the room.

The boat could now be clearly seen from the top of the cliff above the lagoon. They recognized it as one of the armored sampans that had left the evening before with Stürmer and his men, but it was still too far away to see anyone on board except the head and shoulders of the helmsman.

Hazzard went down the wide path to the wharf where people were beginning to gather and wait for the sampan to enter the quiet waters of the cove. A group of women and children hovered behind the men, and Hazzard knew by their expressions these were the families of some of the men who had gone out with Stürmer.

The steady throb of the boat's engine grew louder, and it cut swiftly into view in the small opening between the rock walls. Three soldiers were standing along the sides with long poles in their hands, and as the helmsman cut the engine, they began to pole the boat through the shallow water. It came toward the wharf at an agonizingly slow pace. There were no calls or questions from the shore. The sight of the bullet-torn superstructure was evidence enough that few men on the boat were alive, and that the other boat would never be seen again.

Ropes were thrown and the sampan was pulled up and secured to the wharf. Hazzard stepped forward until he could look down into the sunken deck between the steel-sided gunwales. The wounded lay or sat on one side, and the dead were lined up in a neat row on the other, some of them covered, and others exposed to the harsh rays of the sun. Dried blood, spent cartridges, and discarded weapons littered the open spaces of the deck. The unarmored superstructure was honeycombed with bullet holes and ragged spaces where the wood had splintered off under the impact of the intense firing.

It was a sickening sight of blood and carnage, of defeat and disillusionment, and Hazzard felt he himself was partially to blame for not having completed his mission of discovering the spy.

Men were helping the wounded from the boat, and as Hazzard walked forward to give them a hand, he saw Moro sitting in a small pit by the helm with Stürmer's head cradled in his lap. Hazzard leaped into the boat, and kneeling next to Moro, he lifted the bloody rag from Stürmer's face. He winced at the sight of the blood oozing up through the raw flesh across the German's eyes.

"Doctor Kelly!" he called out. "Come here! It's Stürmer!"

Kelly looked up from where he was examining the wounded, barked instructions at some soldiers standing near him, and jumped into the sampan beside Stürmer.

The doctor took one look at the ugly wound and yelled at two men, who were lifting a dead body out of the boat. They set the body down and hopped quickly into the open pit next to the doctor. He told them in rapid Vietnamese to carry Stürmer to the hospital and then climbed back onto the wharf.

Hazzard jumped up beside him and watched the two soldiers carefully carry the limp form of Stürmer up the path.

"Will he live?" he asked the doctor.

Kelly reached down to grab the bottle of whisky he had been using to sterilize some of the minor cuts on the wounded and took a long drink.

"Yes, he'll live," Kelly said as he wiped his mouth with the back of his hand. "But he'll never see again."

He held the bottle up again to finish the last of the whisky. Then, heaving the empty bottle out into the lagoon, he followed the long line of wounded up the steep path.

Moro climbed slowly and wearily from the sampan. Clutched in his hand was the bloodstained cap Stürmer had always worn, and in his eyes was the deep smouldering fire of hatred that would glow until the day it burst into the flame of ruthless revenge.

The next afternoon Hazzard went to see Stürmer. He had just mounted the steps of the hospital when doctor Kelly came out, wiping the sweat from his face with a dirty piece of gauze.

"It always gets hot like this just before the rainy season," he remarked when he saw Hazzard.

"How is he?" asked Hazzard.

Kelly sat on the split bamboo railing and lit a cigarette. "He's all right, except for the fact he'll be blind for the rest of his life." He paused to study the cigarette in his hand. "And something else has happened to him—inside. It's strange, but the bitterness he had before is gone."

"The bitterness is gone?" Hazzard repeated.

"I know what you're thinking. A thing like this, suddenly becoming blind, would normally make a man bitter, especially a man like Stürmer. But it seems to be having a reverse effect on him. I don't think anyone will ever be able to figure out just what goes on inside a human being."

"What's going to happen to him now?" Hazzard asked.

"It's like a pair of shoes. When they get old and useless, nobody wants them anymore. So, you just throw them on the trash heap, forget them, and go get a new pair." Kelly paused to crush the cigarette beneath his heel. "You can go in and see him if you want," and he walked down the steps, wiping his face and neck with the small piece of gauze.

Sheets had been hung from ropes around the area of Stürmer's bed to wall him off from the pitiful sight of the other sick and wounded without giving thought to the fact he could not see. Hazzard pushed the stained sheets aside and stepped into the small enclosure. Stürmer was lying on his back, his eyes heavily bandaged, and his hands folded peacefully across his chest. Under the window squatted the small form of Moro, still clutching the German army cap in his hands, and staring blankly at the floor. He gave no outward indication he had noticed Hazzard, who now stood quietly at the foot of the bed.

Stürmer moved his head as he seemed to sense the presence of someone else. "Who is it?" he asked.

"It's me, Hazzard."

"Ah, Herr Hazzard." Stürmer smiled and patted the bed with his hand. "Come, sit."

Hazzard unbuttoned the pocket of his shirt and took out the cord and key. "I've come to . . ."

"You are my first visitor. Sit here," and Stürmer patted the bed again.

Hazzard sat on the edge of the mattress, and Stürmer folded his hands across his chest again.

"Lying here like this gives a man much time to think. Last

night I lay awake for a long time. It is surprising I had never noticed the many sounds of the jungle before. We rely on our eyes
too much for beauty. There is much beauty to be found in the
sounds around us. Something which we human beings seldom
appreciate." Stürmer paused and thought of Hazzard sitting and
watching him. "You are wondering why I am not feeling sorry for
myself."

Hazzard was beginning to feel uneasy. "Why, no I . . ."

"Please, do not feel sorry for me, Herr Hazzard. To understand
me you must first know something about me. Many years ago,
during the war, I was a colonel in the German army. I became
wounded in Africa, and after my release from the hospital, I was
second in command of a prison camp in Germany."

"You don't have to tell me," interrupted Hazzard.

"No, it is all right. I feel I must tell someone. It is good to talk
about it after keeping it inside me for so many years," and he
paused to arrange his thoughts. "At first, I thought I was going to
a camp for prisoners of war, but I found they were all political
prisoners and Jewish people the Third Reich had decided were too
dangerous to the government to be allowed to walk around freely.
At first it was not so bad, but as the war steadily went against us,
we began to receive orders to exterminate the prisoners. A large
building was converted into an airtight gas chamber, and ten gas-
fired furnaces were constructed to cremate the bodies. Every day
the orders increased, until finally the gas chamber and the furnaces were in constant use, twenty-four hours a day."

Stürmer had begun to breathe heavily, his words coming faster
as he began to relive the horrible scenes again in his memory.

"Women, children, even small babies. There were no excep-
tions. It became such that I could not sleep. The camp doctor gave
me medicine, and then when I slept, I would see them, slowly
walking by, and as they passed, their eyes would look up at me,
empty and hollow. They seemed to be asking me why this was
happening to them. Even I could not answer."

He reached out a searching hand, found Hazzard's arm, and

grabbed his wrist in a firm grip. "Soon, the war came close, and we could hear the artillery firing in the distance. The guards began to desert until there was no one left except the prisoners, the commanding officer, and myself."

His voice dropped and he relaxed his grip on Hazzard's arm. "He shot himself in the head with his pistol. That night I left. I changed to civilian attire, made my way to friends in the Bavarian Alps, and lost myself among the confusion of returning refugees and soldiers. Later, after the war was over, I learned I was wanted as a criminal for war crimes. I changed my name and went to Africa. The Arab nations were very sympathetic to the German cause, and I found work and settled down to a peaceful life. But it was not as peaceful as I had hoped. Over the years, the scenes in that camp kept returning to haunt me. I had to find something to atone for what I had done. I became a wandering mercenary soldier. Then, one day, I was approached by Herr Chang, and he told me of the situation here. I felt if I could come and help, I could somehow look my God in the face. Now, I am happy. God has punished me far more than man could. It is so easy to die. To live is the challenge. I know now if I do not despair, or curse God for this affliction, then I shall be able to live as a man, and die peacefully when the time comes."

Stürmer stopped talking and folded his hands over his chest again. Hazzard sat for a long time looking at the bandaged face. What does a man say when he has looked into the secrets of another man's soul? He placed the cord and key in Stürmer's hand, patted him lightly on the shoulder and left. There are no words to say good-bye in situations like this.

*   *   *

16.

THE ENEMY COMES

Captain Chen was extremely happy over his victory in the battle with the raiders. Though one of the enemy's boats had managed to slip out of the narrow bay and disappear into the darkness, taking the foreign leader with it, he had captured eleven of them alive. Four of these were too badly wounded to attend to at the limited facilities of Thai-Binh, and deciding they would never live through the rugged trip to Hanoi, Captain Chen ordered they be humanely put to rest—by a firing squad. He also thought it would be a splendid psychological stroke to allow the other seven prisoners to watch the executions. It might make them more talkative when they were questioned.

The wounded raiders were carried to the warehouse area where they were forced to stand while Chen's men strapped them to posts with telephone wire.

The remaining prisoners were lined up along one side, each with his hands tied tightly behind his back, and strung together by telephone wire that had been looped from each one's wrists to the neck of the one behind.

Captain Chen stood before them and gave the little speech he always had ready for such occasions. He said they were about to witness the penalty of the People's Court that was invariably handed down to those who committed high treason.

By experience, Captain Chen knew if the executions were completed swiftly, they would lose their effect upon the seven survivors, and so, he ordered the firing squad to shoot one man at a time.

Purposely, he dragged out the periods between each killing by casually walking up to each corpse and examining it for a long time. He then ordered the dead body taken away. Two of his soldiers would then grab the corpse by its feet and drag it slowly past the remaining prisoners.

In his demented mind, Captain Chen could not conceive these actions could possibly have a reverse effect upon the prisoners. To him, it was the easiest way to grease stubborn tongues into talkativeness. But to the seven Vietnamese, this fat, greasy little man, who strutted before them, was more than an enemy of war. He was Chinese. An alien from another country that had brought many years of suffering to the land they had sweated over so long to gain freedom and independence from French rule. Chen was a living symbol of all they hated, and with each volley of shots, their jaws closed tighter.

After the executions, Captain Chen interrogated the prisoners. Each of them just stood and seemed to look through him with blank, unwavering, emotionless eyes. When the fifth prisoner had stood for five minutes before him like a deaf-mute, Captain Chen's frustration reached its limit.

"Take him out and shoot him!" he screamed.

Again the prisoners were lined up to watch the killing of another comrade. The fat, little officer paced up and down before them, promising the same fate to all if they did not talk.

After the body had been dragged before them, he walked up to the first prisoner in line. He asked one question.

"How many men are there at Tu-Hao-Tuc?"

The prisoner stared into space above the little officer's head. "Shoot him!" cried Chen.

The prisoner was cut loose from the others, tied to a post and shot.

One by one the prisoners were asked the same question, and one by one they were hauled away to meet their fate before the rifles of the firing squad.

As Chen stood before the last remaining prisoner, he leaned within an inch of the man's face and screamed the question.

"How many men at Tu-Hao-Tuc?"

The prisoner looked down into the pudgy eyes of the captain, and spit full in his face. Chen leaped back, cursing the prisoner in Chinese, and drawing his revolver, he shot the man three times in the face. The body collapsed forward at his feet, and Chen deliberately bent down and shot into the back of the man's head.

Walking briskly back to the garrison commander's small office, he ordered one of the soldiers to clean his blood spattered boots. While this was being done, he hurriedly conferred with his junior officers. They would leave immediately, traveling southward along the coastal road in an effort to recover the time lost in repelling the raiders.

The commander of the Thai-Binh garrison was relieved and happy to see the four companies depart, though they had left him with eleven more bodies to bury. Having a man like Captain Chen in his area was highly demoralizing, not only to himself, but to his men as well. Now, he could settle down again to his peaceful routine of guarding the warehouses, and taking forty per cent of the fishermen's catch as token payment for keeping peace in the village.

*   *   *

Captain Chen kept his men moving quickly and steadily down the coast. They marched for two hours, then rested for fifteen minutes. At night they stopped only long enough to cook a supply of rice to last them through the next day. He knew he was pushing the men unmercifully, and he gloated over their suffering as they staggered along the dusty road under the blazing tropical sun. They would have enough time to rest while they were waiting for the reconnaissance patrol to return.

Fifteen miles north of Tu-Hao-Tuc he turned his column east into the jungle. Here they made camp and set up a strong perimeter defense. Being this close to the guerrilla headquarters, there was the constant danger of a sudden surprise attack.

Chen now decided he himself would lead the reconnaissance patrol. He could judge the area and defenses first hand, and thereby save valuable time in planning the strategy of his attack.

He chose twelve men to go with him. Four of them from his own special troops to carry the radio so he could constantly be in touch with Hanoi.

They had been picking their way quietly southward through the jungle for eight hours when they came to a large and aged mahogany tree. After the last man had passed, the noises of the jungle that had hushed at the presence of the intruders, came slowly back to life. The branches of the tree stirred slightly as if in the wind, but there was no wind. Then, a deeply tanned Vietnamese boy dropped soundlessly to the ground and faded quickly away among the trees.

*   *   *

Hazzard was watching his men being put through a set of rugged calisthenics by Big Stoop, who was now first sergeant of the group, when he noticed Chang hurrying along the jungle path toward him.

"I have just received word a patrol of thirteen North Vietnamese is headed in this direction," Chang told him. "They are less than twenty miles away. I do not know why such a small group is in this area. Either they have lost their way, or more likely, they think a few troops can infiltrate and check our defenses. Whatever their objective is, they must be intercepted."

Hazzard looked at him slyly. He knew Chang had not come rushing out into the jungle to tell him this as idle conversation. "And who is going to do the intercepting?" he asked.

"I thought maybe you would like to go," said Chang. "You have been wanting a bit of action, and this is something that should not take you more than four days to complete."

"And give me a chance to see what my boys can do," said Hazzard as he looked toward where his men were doing deep knee bends with their rifles held behind their necks.

"No, I am afraid you cannot use your men. You will have to take others who have had long experience in this type of fighting," replied Chang. "I do not want them all killed off. I must have prisoners, and to do that you must take them by surprise. I will pick the men who will go. They will be the best."

Hazzard was disappointed, but he knew better than to argue with Chang. "All right. When do I leave?"

"You will have to leave tomorrow morning. We will assemble at six o'clock in the clearing at the bayonet course." Chang began to wonder if asking Hazzard to go had been the right thing to do. "There is one more thing you must know. Although you will act as the leader, you must let the men handle the situation in their own way."

"Just going along for the ride, eh?" grinned Hazzard. "Okay, at least it'll be something different. I don't seem to be doing much around here anyway."

After Chang left, Hazzard dismissed the men and wandered aimlessly about the area. The subject of the mysterious spy was bothering him more than ever, especially since he had seen Stürmer in the hospital. He had checked on the movements of Kelly after the doctor had left the villa the night they had decided on the plans for Stürmer's raid, and he was convinced the doctor could not have sent any messages from Tu-Hao-Tuc. This did not eliminate Kelly from the suspect list, but you just did not go around openly accusing people without solid, concrete proof.

He was sitting among the rocks that lay scattered about on

top of the high bluff overlooking the sea when he heard heavy footsteps in the loose shale behind him. The massive form of Ming Lee suddenly loomed into view and lumbered toward him. Instinctively Hazzard glanced about for an escape route. He did not trust the simple mentality of the giant, and it would be suicide trying to fight off any mayhem the gorilla-like Ming Lee might possibly be contemplating for some unknown reason.

When he saw Hazzard, Ming Lee's stony face twitched into a weird grimace. Hazzard did not know for sure, but he thought the giant was trying to smile. It was a gesture of friendliness the big man was totally unfamiliar with, and as he came forward, he held out a piece of paper. Hazzard unfolded it, and saw it was a note from Ling Ling Yung. He looked up again, but the giant was gone.

The note was penned in finely shaped characters:

> Dear Mr. Hazzard,
> I wish to see you. Please come tonight at eight o'clock.
> Ming Lee will bring you through the guard posts.
>
>   Ling Ling Yung

Hazzard toyed with the idea of not going. Why become involved with this beautiful woman who was so desirable, yet so inaccessible? Then he folded the note away in his pocket. Stop kidding yourself Hazzard. He remembered something he had learned in Japanese language school about the ancient samurai. Never refuse the proffered dish. He smiled as he looked at his watch. Eight o'clock? He would be there.

That evening, Ming Lee had met Hazzard on the path leading up the slope to the villa. He had followed the giant past the heavily armed guards and been shown into a room he had never seen before. There was less furniture than the overstuffed room where they had held their conferences. A low table, a few chairs, and a luxuriously padded king-size divan covered with soft pillows. Hazzard had been left by himself, and he sat on the divan, gazing absentmindedly around the room. He noticed the round Chinese-style windows were fitted with frames of milky white paper that allowed light to filter into the room, but prevented anyone from seeing either in or out. On the inside of the only door was a heavy brass bolt. Hazzard decided the room had been constructed to allow the utmost in privacy, and the thought made his flesh tingle with a spasm of short-lived goose pimples.

The door opened and a boy brought in a tray with an ornate teapot, cups, and the remainder of the bottle of French cognac that had been opened the night before Stürmer had left on his ill-fated raid.

After the boy left, Hazzard did not know whether he was supposed to help himself or wait until Ling Ling made her appearance. He had just made up his mind his constitution needed a little courage from the brandy when the door opened again and a radiant Ling Ling slipped into the room. She softly shut the door and leaned back against it.

"Thank you very much for coming," she said in her throaty voice and came across the room to sit next to Hazzard. Without another word she poured two cups of tea and surprised Hazzard by lacing each one heavily with the cognac. She handed him a cup and they drank in silence. The hot tea and brandy settled warmly in his stomach, and Hazzard knew Ling Ling was feeling the same sensation.

As he tilted his head back to drain the last of the aromatic tea, his eyes focused on the door, and the goose-pimple sensation returned. The brass bolt had been slipped into place. They were now locked in the room together. A locked room, a bottle of brandy, and a beautiful woman. Hazzard thought about the heated kiss and began to wonder what was expected of him now. He wanted this woman's respect, but he also had an overpowering desire for her body.

She put her cup down, and was so close Hazzard could feel the soft caress of her breath on his cheek as she spoke.

"Chang has told me you are going into the jungle tomorrow." Hazzard nodded. "You must promise me to be very careful." Her voice had taken on a different tone now, and Hazzard turned his head to look into her dark, anxious eyes.

It was the same as the last time, an impulse impossible to deny. His arms went around her, his lips found hers, and as they relaxed into each others embrace, they slumped sideways to the softness of the divan. The next time she spoke, her lips were close to his, her eyes searching and memorizing every detail of his face, her perfume drifting intoxicatingly across the downy pillows.

"Tell me, how many women have you kissed?"

"I have kissed many before, but I have never kissed a woman like this," and he placed one hand in the small of her back and pulled her close. Their mouths met, and he forced her's open with his tongue. She stiffened momentarily, and then pressed her body up against his while her hands dug frantically at his back.

She had never known such ecstasy before. He kissed her mouth, her eyes, her cheek. A tremor ran through her body, awakening the passion that had lain dormant all these years as his lips found the softness of her neck and his tongue caressed her quivering throat.

The room darkened into night and they surrendered slowly to their desires, each becoming bolder as they loosened catches and buttons that hindered their exploring hands. The clothes of convention lay unwanted by their sides as their bodies melted into one and the storm of passion reached its climax to gradually subside into the soft murmurs and caresses of rapturous contentment.

*   *   *

17.
A TASTE OF BLOOD

When Hazzard awoke the next morning, he lay staring at the monotony of the mosquito netting above his head. The memory of Ling Ling was like an impossible dream come true. He breathed in heavily and found the scent of her perfume still lingered with him.

It was five o'clock, and swinging his feet out from under the netting, he sat on the edge of the bed. If he never had another woman for the rest of his life, he would now be able to die a satisfied man.

The sudden thought of dying snapped his brain back to the realities that confronted him. He was about to take off into the jungle to search for a communist patrol. A jungle about which he knew almost nothing, and to depend upon jungle tactics about which he was equally ignorant. He tried to create a reason for having so readily agreed to go, and as he dressed, he amused himself with the thought he subconsciously wanted to do his share by taking part in the sacrificing struggle that was going on around him daily. Or perhaps it was a death wish that lay dormant somewhere in the back of his mind. Actually, he knew the real reason, but hesitated to admit it even to himself. It was Stürmer. Seeing the man lying there, doomed to a life of darkness, and yet believing he was better off now than before was something Hazzard wondered if he himself could do, if ever the circumstances were reversed, and it was he who lay there. Now it was becoming a personal matter. He would catch the spy, but first—a taste of blood.

He finished dressing and checked Sam to make sure there were no rust spots forming anywhere on the well-oiled steel. Satisfied, he pushed the pistol into his waistband and stuffed the small leather pouch of 357 magnum shells into his pocket.

The gray streaks of dawn were just beginning to appear above the trees as he set the bush hat at a jaunty angle on his head, winked at himself in the mirror, and stepped out into the large room of the quarters. The others were still sleeping, but the noisy sounds of early morning life came to him from the direction of the village—the chopping of wood, the barking of a dog, the banging of a metal pan, the occasional cry of a hungry baby. He shivered against the coolness of the early morning mist and the dampness of his clothes. Pausing only long enough to select the ripest banana from a large bunch on the end of the long table, he walked out into the compound and turned toward the area where the patrol would be assembling.

Chang was speaking French to the men who would make up the small expedition when Hazzard arrived. There were ten of them standing in a line. As soldiers, they appeared to be the best selection of misfits Hazzard had ever seen. They stood listening to Chang, wearing a variety of items from uniforms to rags. Some bareheaded, some with filthy wraps of cloth that imitated poor attempts at winding turbans, and two of them, for some unexplained reason, wore the green berets of the French Foreign Legion. The weapons they carried were as varied as the clothing. British Enfields, German Mausers, American Garands, one or two communist rifles of Russian origin, and one rusted weapon that had once belonged to the Japanese Imperial Army. A few of them had pistols and grenades, and all of them carried lethal, wicked-looking, razor sharp knives hanging from their belts.

Hazzard smiled and thought of their resemblance to a gang of Oriental pirates that could only have been created in a Milton Caniff comic strip.

Chang finished talking and turned to Hazzard. "These are the men who will go with you. Each one is an experienced jungle fighter. You can rely on them to do their job thoroughly and quickly."

Hazzard only nodded and moved off toward the line of men. As he approached, one of them called everyone to attention. Stiffly, and somewhat comically, they came to various poses each thought was the most efficient military stance. Hazzard no longer smiled. He knew these men, as comical as they appeared, were more deadly than a pool full of blood-crazed sharks. Slowly he moved down the line looking into each face and glancing over the fighting equipment they carried. The clothes were dirty, the faces unshaven, the bandoliers of cartridges crusted with jungle rot, the bodies reeking of sweat, the rifles rusted and pitted, but the look in their eyes was purposeful and deadly.

Glancing at one badly rusted German Mauser, that probably had not seen a drop of oil since 1945, he thought of the stern military commanders who would have had ulcers at the sight of such weapons, and of the unmerciful punishment they would have dealt out to the hapless soldier.

He also remembered a time in Korea when he had been visiting an American military advisory group at one of the ROK division headquarters. A truck load of captured Russian-made weapons had just been brought in from the forward companies and were laying in disordered piles in front of the tents. The weapons had been crudely manufactured and now lay rusted and mud caked, many held together by bits of wire and nails. One young, fresh from school, American second lieutenant looked at the piles of weapons in disgust. "Well, the Russians sure aren't doing them any favors giving them this kind of junk to fight with," he remarked aloud.

The senior KMAG officer, an experienced American infantry major, had cut him off with the humorless reply, "Maybe not, but this junk can still kill a hell of a lot of people."

Hazzard felt the same way now. In spite of their rough, shoddy appearance, he could not have picked a better group himself. He was pleased with Chang's choice until he came to the last man, and suddenly found himself looking down into the upturned, grinning face of a young teen-age boy.

"Chang!" he called out. "Come here!"

The boy grinned and bowed slightly as Chang stopped beside the tall American leader who wore the wonderful hat.

"What's this kid doing here?" asked Hazzard. "I can't take him with me."

"This is Lin. He will be your guide."

"Now look, Chang, let's not get ridiculous about this . . ."

Chang held up a hand to stop him. "He is quite experienced at this sort of thing, even though he is only fifteen. The men trust him, and so do I. Besides, he speaks a few words of English, and none of the others do. You have no choice. It has already been decided."

Hazzard was about to protest again but he saw by the look in Chang's eyes it would be useless. He looked back at Lin and found he could not stop the smile that came to his lips as he gazed at the boy's infectious grin. Shaking his head in resignation to the unfathomable Oriental mind, he decided to accept the inevitable.

"Do these other boys know what we're supposed to do?" Hazzard asked.

"They have all been briefed on what has to be done. Lin, here, knows where they were last seen. In fact, he is the one who originally discovered them," Chang replied matter-of-factly.

This caused Hazzard to look with new interest at the eternally grinning boy who stood before him. Chang dug into his pocket and handed Hazzard a small packet wrapped in oilcloth.

"In case you should get separated from the others, here is a map and compass. It is best to make your way to the sea and follow the coastline if you become lost."

"Okay," said Hazzard as he took the packet and stuffed it into his back pocket. Then turning to the young boy, "Well, Lin, you're the one who knows the way, so let's get this show on the road."

Lin's smile faded and his brow puckered up into little wrinkles. "Show?" he queried.

"It means, it is time to go," and Hazzard patted him on the head.

The grin immediately returned as Lin understood. "Yes, yes. We go now."

The rest of them fell in behind Hazzard without a word as Lin led the column across the clearing and away from the village.

The outward attitude of the men seemed to change as they stepped into the jungle. They tensed, but moved with the agility and silence of jungle cats. Hazzard felt guilty and self-conscious every time he made a noise or stepped on a crackling dead branch, but the men appeared not to notice. Slowly, by constantly watching the others, he began to learn, and the more he learned, the quieter his movements became.

They kept up a slow, methodical pace until they halted on the side of a hill six hours later. Lin carried on a long animated conversation with the men, using a stick to draw lines on the ground that Hazzard assumed was a crude map. Dried food and water were then passed among the men, and they ate in silence. When the journey began again, Hazzard saw the order of march had changed, and now, two of the men walked well ahead, out of sight, but leaving silent markers in the jungle for the others to follow.

The pace continued without a halt. It was not fast, but the constant push through the jungle was something Hazard was not accustomed to, and he began to tire rapidly. They halted for the second time just before dusk, and Hazzard let himself collapse and sprawl unashamedly on the thick leaf bedding of the jungle floor. He had no idea of where they were, nor how far they had traveled, and at this particular moment, he could not have cared less.

Lin squatted beside him to explain in his limited English, and with the help of a map drawn in the dirt with sticks, the position they were now at, and that they probably would make contact with the communist patrol sometime during the afternoon of the following day. All Lin's calculations were based upon the original position where he had seen the enemy, together with their speed and direction of march, compared to the speed and direction Hazzard's little band had come through the jungle. The plan was to set up an ambush and wait until the Red soldiers walked into it. It all sounded so simple. To Lin and the others it was just an odd job that had to be done. Hazzard was not convinced it would be as easy as Lin made it appear, but he kept silent and only nodded his understanding of what the boy said.

Glancing about, Hazzard found himself looking at these men with a new-found admiration. So far they had gone about their business with an efficiency that would be hard to find in the best-disciplined troops of any Western army. There was no grumbling, no arguing, in fact, there was very little conversation. Each seemed to know exactly what was expected of him, and the whole group moved with a teamwork and silence that was as cold and deadly as it was efficient. Hazzard could not help thinking he was glad they were on his side, but he also wondered if the enemy patrol they would meet tomorrow might not be just as efficient. If they were, then this could turn out to be an Oriental "Custer's Last Stand" for both sides.

He turned to look at the strange young dark-eyed boy who squatted beside him. Lin was gazing at him with his constantly smiling face. Hazzard returned the grin and wondered what it was that sent this boy out to war when he should have been in school somewhere, or at least sitting in his family's hut helping with the chores.

"Lin," he said slowly so the boy would understand. "You are very young to be doing this kind of work. Aren't you afraid?"

The grin vanished, and he sat up straight with pride and anger. "No. No afraid," he said hotly.

"Oh, don't get angry now. I didn't mean to insult you," and Hazzard's mind gave him a mental kick. God, these Orientals.

You had to be on your toes every second. "I just wanted to know why you were doing this—guiding patrols through the jungle."

The boy looked at him for a long moment while he digested Hazzard's last words. Then his body relaxed and the smile returned. "I will be leader someday," he said slowly as he carefully picked his words. "People follow because I brave. Now I young, I learn what is to be leader."

"I understand," Hazzard nodded and a long period of silence followed. Hazzard could not think of anything to say to continue the conversation along these lines, and he was reluctant to change the subject for fear of upsetting the boy again.

Lin took a deep breath, and looking up at Hazzard, he began to speak again. "Someday, when I leader . . ." He paused to think of words and pointed to the bush hat on Hazzard's head. "I wear same same hat. People look. People know I leader." He stopped and let the air gush out of his lungs in a sigh from the effort of, what was to Lin, a long speech.

This line of thinking amazed Hazzard, who could not for the life of him imagine what a hat had to do with the making of a leader of men. Was it Oriental logic beating again at his Occidental-trained mind, or was it just the thoughts and dreams of a young boy?

"So, you want to wear a hat like this?" he said as he removed the bush hat from his head. He looked at the hat in his hands for a few seconds, and then he decided. He reached out and put it on the boy's head.

Lin stiffened momentarily, then his eyes widened in surprise and his hands shot up to caress the hat. Then, just as quickly, his mood changed and he looked at Hazzard with disbelief. "I . . . I wear hat?" he asked in a hushed voice.

"Yep, you wear it for a while and see how you like it," replied Hazzard.

The moon had now come up and Hazzard glanced at the luminous dial of his watch. "Right now, let's get some sleep. We've got a rough day tomorrow."

Lin had taken the hat off and was absorbed in admiring it when Hazzard spoke. He only clearly heard and understood the word 'sleep', and nodded. Hazzard wrapped his head in the light jacket he had remembered to bring and was soon asleep.

The moon rose high in the dark, clear tropical sky. The sounds of the jungle at night, of unseen insects and animals, rose and fell softly, and Lin stayed awake, deaf and blind to all that was around him except the wonderful hat he held in his hands.

*   *   *

Captain Chen had received an urgent radio message from Hanoi telling him his patrol had been spotted, and a group of men were on their way to intercept him. This had caused him to keep the men moving during the night without rest. He knew now the spy they had so carefully planted in Tu-Hao-Tuc was still alive and active, but after the nest of traitors was exterminated, the spy would be of no further use. Having previously made up his mind to execute the spy if they found him alive, he could now find no logical reason for changing his decision and mentally shrugged off the informer as an expendable item of war.

They paused for a short rest just before dawn, and at the first touch of grayness in the eastern sky, they started out again. The day was a repetition of the one before. The silent, steady pace, the sun, the heat, and the constant monotony of the jungle.

At noon they had come to a small cleared space cut through the jungle like a firebreak, and they stopped again. Captain Chen stretched out beneath a large tree to consult a map of the area, and to enjoy one of the few remaining American cigarettes he had found on the dead body of one of the prisoners. The pleasant aroma seeped through his nostrils, and he remembered the last time he had been fortunate enough to taste this fragrant tobacco. It had been the day he had successfully ambushed a company of green South Vietnamese soldiers a foolish American sergeant had taken into the jungle on a training mission. He smiled at the recollection. It had been ridiculously easy. The South Vietnamese soldiers had been thrown into confusion. The GI had been cut almost in two by a machine gun burst as he stood shouting unheeded orders to his men. Luckily, the bullets had spared the package of cigarettes in the sergeant's pocket.

He looked about, and mentally counted the men scattered under the trees and bushes. Eleven including himself, and the two forward scouts made up thirteen. He had carefully chosen the men, and he smiled at his wisdom, for no one had ever told him 13 was an unlucky number. In not knowing about a superstition, one should be safe from it; or so it would seem.

The efficiency of his men was well displayed as one of the forward scouts came running back to report the presence of an armed band of eleven men headed in their direction. This could only be the patrol he had been warned about. His first thought was to annihilate them swiftly and continue with his mission of scouting the defenses of the coastal village, but the message had said they were being led by a foreigner, and a new idea began to germinate in Chen's brain.

He would capture this foreign bandit alive, and then there would be no further reason to go closer to the village. The natives would be eliminated as it would be impossible to get them to talk, but the foreigner—yes, he would talk. He smiled at the thought of the methods he would use, and of his triumphal return. He would have all the information he desired. Also, if the foreigner was not a weak one, he would have a strange prize to show off and help elevate his status.

He questioned the forward scout and formed his plans. The men of the light machine gun crew were given their orders. Then, he personally instructed each of the others as he deployed them through the jungle. When he was finished, he was proud of his work. Yes, Colonel Wu had chosen him well, he thought. He was the master of any situation. The jungle was silent around him as he slipped in among the tangled vines and undergrowth and lay full length beside the machine gunners. The signal for the attack would be the firing of the gun by his side, and now, he settled down to wait, content with the knowledge of what was to come. Motionless as a spider that knows the fly will soon be enveloped in the web.

*   *   *

Hazzard's group had been up and moving since dawn. They had traveled steadily without pausing. Hazzard's muscles, stiff from sleeping on the jungle floor, and still aching from the previous day's march, responded slowly to his will and found himself again making the jungle ring to the noise of his clumsy feet.

Suddenly, Lin raised his hand and every man in the column behind him froze instantly—except Hazzard, who had not expected the signal and was taken by surprise. They had come to a clearing in the jungle and the scouts were crouching low, peering through the heavy foliage at the jungle on the far side of the open space. They remained in this position for almost five minutes, then quickly one of them darted out and ran swiftly and silently across the clearing. Nothing happened, and after another long, silent wait, the second man left as quickly and as quietly as the first. The men behind Hazzard remained motionless, but he could see their eyes darting back and forth as they searched the jungle around them for some hidden clue to a possible enemy.

Soon, one of the scouts reappeared from the jungle on the other side and silently signaled with his arm. Lin stood up from the squatting position he had assumed when they had halted, and the column started moving forward again.

As Hazzard stepped out from the jungle, he looked around on both sides and thought how the cleared spaced resembled the fire-breaks he had once seen cut through the forests in the mountains of Oregon.

Lin was almost halfway across the clearing when Hazzard looked up at a noise above his head and saw a comical looking parrot fly mockingly by. He was just about to wink humorously at the crazy bird when his feet became entangled in a vine and he started to fall. As he hit the ground Hazzard heard both the machine gun and Lin's hoarse cry.

The air was now filled with the popping sound of rifle fire and the slick cutting hiss of bullets as they sliced through the thick grass and leaves.

Hazzard cautiously raised his head. A thin veil of smoke hung about the jungle in front of him, but whoever was doing the firing was smart enough to remain well back from the edge of the clearing so the jungle foliage would hide the muzzle flashes. He lowered his head and began to crawl forward. Somewhere ahead of him was Lin, and he knew the boy had been hit. He had heard that cry before. In France, in Germany, in Korea, and other places long forgotten. The sound that comes involuntarily to a man's throat as a bullet tears through the body, expanding, and smashing him to the ground.

He found Lin lying on his side. Blood trickling from the corner of his mouth. The bush hat clenched tightly in his fist, and wheezing from the hole the bullet had bored through his chest and lung.

Hazzard tore a strip of cloth from the tail of his shirt and tied the boy's wrists together. Rolling Lin carefully on his back, Hazzard stuck his head through the boy's bound arms, and began the long crawl back to the safety of the jungle, dragging the boy along beneath him.

Hazzard had lost all thought of the other members of his group since the firing had started. Now, as he crawled slowly along, he realized the firing was only coming from the other side, and he suddenly remembered he had not heard any return fire from his men since they had been attacked. He now began to have misgivings about these men, whom he had thought were so tough and deadly. He remembered stories of other ambushes in the jungle, of how the men fled from the scene at the first sign of danger. He did not want to believe this about these men he had admired, but where were they now? Why hadn't they returned the fire?

Lin's head struck the ground as Hazzard's elbow slipped on the slick grass. He looked down and the boy grinned back. Christ, only fifteen, and what a way to die, he thought. He smiled back at the boy and continued crawling through the deep grass toward the jungle, cursing the men who had so quickly disappeared.

Hazzard did not know it at the time, but his fears were groundless, and he would later feel ashamed at his quick damnation of the men Chang had so carefully chosen.

The men were long experienced at this type of jungle ambush. Not that the suddenness of it had not taken them by surprise, but at the instant of it's happening, they knew at once what to do, and went about their business with a lethal thoroughness.

Even as Hazzard was crawling forward in search of Lin, they had melted into the jungle. Now, they were appearing again as if by magic, singly and in pairs. The members of Chen's patrol became conscious of their presence only when their heads were jerked swiftly backwards and the cold sensation of razor sharp steel momentarily touched their throats to be followed by the warm flow of blood and the sudden darkness of eternal night.

Captain Chen listened to the diminishing fire from his left and became grimly aware the enemy was moving silently through the thick undergrowth on his flanks and rear. There was only one thing to do; move forward across the clearing toward the spot where the foreigner had fallen. With him as a prisoner, perhaps the outlaw rabble would give up the fight and run away through the jungle.

He gave the order and two men rose with him as he raced out into the clearing. The machine gunners watched them go and waited to give covering fire if it became necessary.

A shot rang out. The soldier behind Chen buckled without a sound and disappeared into the high grass. They came to the place where Hazzard had hit the ground. Chen cursed and raced across the open space. Suddenly he was alone as one of Hazzard's men leaped up from the concealment of the grass and dragged the remaining soldier to the ground.

Hazzard had reached the jungle, untied the boy's arms, and sat with Lin's head cradled on his leg. The boy still clutched the bush hat and watched Hazzard from behind his never ending grin. The wheezing from his lung was becoming more pronounced and hollow sounding.

Lin licked his lips and tried to speak. Hazzard leaned over closely as faint words came from the boy's blood-flecked mouth.

"They . . . think . . . me . . . leader . . . they see . . . hat . . . they . . . think . . . me . . . leader . . ."

Hazzard looked down at the boy and realized the dream of Lin had been fulfilled. To the boy, death was now nothing. He was dying content with the knowledge he had accomplished his goal in life. He had earned the respect of the enemy as a leader. What greater proof was there than they had shot him down with the first burst of gunfire? It was true the leaders would always be fired at first. Lin was a leader, the enemy had proven it for all to see.

The shrill cry of the machine gunner pierced the jungle air as one of Hazzard's men failed to cut deep enough with the knife. Hazzard jerked his head up at the sound and saw before him the grinning face of Captain Chen Shu Wen.

The sudden appearance of the communist officer startled Hazzard. The fat, greasy face of Chen jolted an almost forgotten memory in the back of Hazzard's brain, and he just sat there, staring in amazement.

Chen knew it would now be impossible to take the tall foreigner prisoner, and so he must die. He did not recognize Hazzard. The memory was lost among the jumble of long-forgotten foreign faces that had never been clearly imprinted upon his memory. He slowly raised his pistol to take careful aim, and mistaking the amazement on Hazzard's face for fear, he was not prepared for the sudden sideward lunge. He turned his body slightly to follow the movement, but he was that fraction of a second that stands between life and death too late.

Captain Chen neither heard the deep sharp crack of Sam's angry muzzle, nor felt the 357 magnum slug when it entered just below his flaring nostrils, went on to fill his brain with bits of finely ground bone, and lifted the top of his skull from his head as it made its hurried exit to soar high above the trees to an unknown destination in the jungle.

Hazzard stood and stared down at the lifeless form of Captain Chen. The eyes were open as though they had been startled by the sudden recognition of a long-forgotten memory. Hazzard, too, was startled. Here before him lay the body of the man he remembered as Lieutenant Chen, the brutal interrogator of the North Korean prisoner of war camps. He also recalled the oath he had sworn long ago. A terrible oath of vengeance. Now, his revenge completed by the unpredictable hand of providence, he felt neither elation or remorse.

His eyes fell upon the single red and yellow ribbon on Chen's tunic. Then, for some unknown reason, Hazzard reached down, unfastened it, and put the ribbon in his pocket. Slowly he turned away from the leering face of what had once been the arrogant Captain Chen, and knelt beside the wounded boy. Hazzard would never know if Lin had seen the death of Captain Chen. The boy's eyes were closed now, and his face held the calm quiet look of those who pass from life in peace.

The jungle was silent again, and Hazzard sat for a long time beside the boy before he became conscious of movement behind him. He spun around to see three of his men standing with a gagged and very frightened prisoner, and he relaxed. It was over now, this deadly business in the jungle.

Silently they returned. Only eight of the men were left. One other, the man who had been directly behind Hazzard as they stepped into the clearing, had been cut down by the first round of firing.

Two of the enemy had been taken prisoner. The others lay where they had fallen. Only their weapons and ammunition had been collected. Lin, the bush hat still held in his stiff, dead hands, and the other man had been buried on the spot. It would have been impossible to carry the bodies for two days through the heat of the jungle.

The prisoners were roped together, and they began the long, silent march back to the village. Hazzard had tasted blood, but the result was not what he had expected. He had come to relieve his bitterness by gambling in the jungle. They had won, but he had forgotten that those who gamble must also be prepared to lose.

*   *   *

18.

AN EYE FOR AN EYE

*T*wo days after Hazzard had returned from the jungle patrol, Chang sent word he wanted to see him at the villa. Hazzard had hoped to see Ling Ling, but Chang was alone in the heavily decorated room. The tall Chinese had just finished a long interview with the two prisoners. They had talked readily after being confronted by the terrible specter of Ming Lee, and now Chang sat at the long carved table with a troubled expression on his face.

"I knew it would come eventually. That patrol was part of a large force camped about twenty-five miles north of here. They were out trying to reconnoiter our defenses," Chang paused, and looked unwavering into Hazzard's eyes. "You did not tell me you killed the officer who was leading them. I do not suppose it will be of much interest to you, but he was Captain Chen Shu Wen, a highly regarded member of the Chinese secret police."

"Yes, I know," Hazzard commented indifferently.

"You know?" said the incredulous Chang.

"I knew Chen when he was only a ratty little lieutenant," explained Hazzard. "He was in charge of the brainwashing when I was a prisoner of war in Korea."

Chang digested this for a moment, and then went on to make his point. "It means they are finally going to attempt to annihilate us completely. I am thankful they have no air force or naval units to use against us."

"And if they come," asked Hazzard. "What do you propose to do? Stand here and fight it out to the last man?"

"No, that would be foolhardy," and going to a large cabinet, Chang withdrew a detailed map of the village area. "Here, I will show you. It is time you knew. I did not think it would become necessary to tell you, but it begins to look like you probably will be here when they come."

He unrolled the map on the table. "This is a map of the village and the immediate surrounding area." As he talked he began to point out various details. "Each building is mined by a large charge of TNT, and various other charges have been placed in the compound, along the streets, and even under this house. They are all connected by electric wires that are marked by these blue lines."

Hazzard noted the positions of the many charges and had the uneasy feeling of suddenly finding out he had been living on top of a gigantic powder keg.

"In the event we are attacked in force by land," continued Chang. "All refugees, women and children, and the sick and wounded will be immediately evacuated by sea. We will fight a delaying action from prepared positions . . . here . . . here . . . and here. When all noncombatants have been evacuated, a red flare will be fired from the cliff above the inlet. This will be the signal for the majority of our troops to disengage and make their way to the boats. Small parties of soldiers will then retreat slowly back through the village. When they have reached the jungle on the far side, they will immediately break off the battle and retreat to the boats. As soon as the enemy has occupied the village, the buried charges will be set off electrically from a point, here, on top of the cliff."

"That's quite a plan," commented Hazzard. "Do you have enough boats to take everyone?"

"Yes, more than enough. We will have to destroy about ten we cannot take with us."

"And where do you plan to go from here if you have to evacuate?" Hazzard asked.

"That is something I cannot tell even you," replied Chang. "Only Ling Ling Yung and myself know. But be assured, we have chosen a very excellent place for a new base of operations."

"Let us hope we shall discover the informer who is in our midst, before we are forced to abandon this village," said the voice of Ling Ling Yung, and Hazzard jerked his head around to see her standing behind his chair. He realized she must have quietly entered the room while he was absorbed in Chang's explanation of the evacuation plan.

Chang came to Hazzard's defense. "I am sure Mr. Hazzard has been doing his best to find the . . ."

"I do not doubt Mr. Hazzard's capabilities," said Ling Ling as she cut off Chang's protest. She tilted her head and smiled down at Hazzard. "We have done nothing constructive to help him. How can we expect someone to assemble a difficult puzzle if we do not give him enough pieces to work with? This informer, whoever he is, is indeed very skillful. I am sure he will eventually be discovered. It is only that I desire to find out who this person is before it is too late." She paused and went to gaze out through the glass-paneled doors. "If only there was some way to set a trap . . ."

The words echoed in Hazzard's brain. A trap! He should have thought of it before. It was the only logical solution. Now, time was fast running out on them. It would have to be done quickly. It might not even work.

Hazzard broke away from his thoughts. "You still need the ammunition Stürmer tried to get, don't you?"

Chang looked puzzled. "Yes, but . . ."

"There must be more than one ammo dump along the coast that could be raided," said Hazzard.

"Mr. Hazzard, do I have to remind you that a large force of communist troops are camped only a short distance north of us," said Chang. "And will probably attack within a few days?"

Hazzard ignored this. "Where's the map you have that shows all their locations?"

"Wait!" said Ling Ling. "I will permit no one to leave here on another mission until the spy has been caught."

Hazzard looked at her and smiled. "No one is going anywhere." Then, he turned to Chang. "Now, can I see the map?"

Chang paused as he looked at Ling Ling, then going to the cabinet, he brought back the large map of the coastal area and spread it across the table.

Hazzard leaned over the map. "Now, show me where these other small depots are located, and then, maybe I'll tell you how we just might catch our spy."

Chang explained the locations of the various ammunition dumps, answered Hazzard's questions, and then both he and Ling Ling listened while Hazzard outlined the plan that had begun to grow in his mind.

"I want you to call a meeting and inform everyone I will be taking a raiding party to the small seaport of Apowan, to raid the small arms depot there. You'll have to call the meeting tonight and announce I will be leaving the day after tomorrow . . . let's say, about nine at night."

Ling Ling started to protest again, but Hazzard raised his hand. "Wait until I've finished, then I don't think you'll have any objections," he told her, and then continued.

"From past experience, our spy, whoever he is, will pass the information on to his commie buddies. By announcing our plans forty-eight hours in advance, it will give them plenty of time to set up an ambush—and I'm almost positive our friend Hanoi Harry will be on the air with it sometime tomorrow night on his seven or eleven o'clock broadcast. We'll get everyone together at the quarters and listen."

"What good will all this do?" broke in Chang.

"You haven't let me finish," smiled Hazzard. "As soon as we hear our friend in Hanoi tell us they have set up an ambush, I will announce to everyone I am not going north to Apowan, but instead, south to Fhu-Dien."

"This is very interesting," remarked Chang. "It will throw the enemy into confusion for a short time, but they will still have twenty-four hours to inform their people at Fhu-Dien of our change in plans."

"Exactly," agreed Hazzard.

"But I do not see how this will help us to catch the spy."

Hazzard leaned back in his chair with a smug look on his face. "If you were the spy, Mr. Chang, what would be your first reaction after I announce my change of plans?"

Chang spoke without hesitation. "I would have to relay this new information to Hanoi as quickly as possible."

"And that, Mr. Chang, is just what I am hoping for. I am going to try and force his hand. He will have to get the new information out fast, and when he moves, he might give himself away. His cover has been excellent so far, but this time he'll be in a hurry, and it's just about time he started getting careless."

Ling Ling regarded Hazzard with anxious eyes. "Then you will not go to either place?"

Hazzard grinned. "No. Why should I? I wasn't hired to go out and capture supplies for you. I was hired to find a spy. So far, I haven't earned my keep, but by tomorrow, maybe I'll have earned the rest of my fee."

*   *   *

Later that night Doctor Kelly, Maurice, Hazzard, and Ling Ling Yung sat at the long teakwood table and listened to Chang outline the details of the raid.

".. . and if all goes well," concluded Chang. "Mr. Hazzard should be back here just before dawn on the following day."

Maurice shook his head in disgust. "I think this is crazy idea. You see what happen to Stürmer."

"There is no possible way for this information to leak out," Chang told them. "Only the five of us know about it."

"Nobody else knew about Stürmer either," commented Kelly.

There was a period of silence, and then Chang asked, "Do any of you have anything else you would like to say?"

No one spoke.

"Then, it is completely settled. Mr. Hazzard will leave here the day after tomorrow at nine in the evening with two motor sampans and forty men. Maurice, you will make sure the sampans are fueled and ready to go, and do it without making the crews ask too many questions."

Maurice shrugged his shoulders. "Oui, I will do this, but I still do not like it."

Chang rolled up the large map and placed it back in the cabinet. The door opened and Wong came in with a large tray covered with cups and a pot of tea.

"Tea? Bah! Too much tannic acid is bad for the stomach," growled Kelly as he took a cup from Wong, and raising it, he glanced around the room. "To the brave, but very foolish Mr. Hazzard.

Hazzard drank with the rest, and wondered just how foolish his idea was. He would know in just about twenty-four hours.

*   *   *

The next day Hazzard took his men out for a session of hand-to-hand combat. He had been there for about two hours, sprawled out in the shade of a large banyan tree, watching the men throw each other about the sand pit, when Chang came along the path from the village and sat beside him.

Neither of them spoke for about ten minutes.

Chang appeared to be nervous over something, but Hazzard decided to conform to the old Oriental custom of patience, and wait for him to open the conversation.

Finally, Chang spoke. "Do you think this plan of yours will work?"

"I don't know," Hazzard replied honestly. "But if I were your spy, it would work on me." He paused and looked sideways at Chang. "What are you so worried about? It's not costing us anything to try."

"It's not that. It is the knowledge that a large force of heavily armed men are camped on our very doorstep, and they could attack us at any moment."

"Why don't you send out some men and harass them? It might discourage them for a while."

"I have learned from the two prisoners that their strength is four full companies. That means there are over one thousand armed men. It would be suicide to send small parties against them. We could never catch them by surprise. They are probably sitting and waiting for us to do just what you suggest."

Hazzard shrugged his shoulders. "What else did you learn from the prisoners?"

"They were the ones who ambushed Herr Stürmer and his raiding party at Thai-Binh."

"Oh? That's interesting."

"More interesting than you think," said Chang, and he related to Hazzard the grisly details surrounding the deaths of the men Chen had captured at Thai-Binh.

Hazzard's blood boiled as he listened to the story. If anyone had ever deserved to die, it had been Chen. It was too bad the fat, greasy little communist officer had been dispatched so quickly and cleanly. For people like Chen, it would be better if death could be slow and agonizing, stretched over a period of days . . . even weeks. Hazzard had had no choice. It had happened too swiftly and without planning. He wondered what he would have done if he had taken Chen alive.

"So you see, Mr. Hazzard, why I am concerned about the presence of a large force of communist troops," concluded Chang. "I do not wish any of the people here to fall into their hands. It would not be pleasant."

"And with an unknown spy running around here freely, it sort of gives them the upper hand," added Hazzard. "Well, Chang, you come over tonight, and we'll all listen to old Hanoi Harry together. If he says what I think he'll say, then we've got a good chance of catching our spy tonight." And to himself he added, "I hope."

*   *   *

Hazzard sat lazily and calmly in one of the creaky bamboo chairs watching Maurice methodically throw darts at the nude poster, and at the same time, wondering if this big, likable French-man could possibly be the mysterious spy.

He moved his eyes to the table where Kelly was silently play-ing solitaire, with the inevitable bottle and glass beside him, and Hazzard let the same thoughts pass through his mind about the doctor.

He glanced at his watch. It was almost seven o'clock. Looking across the room to where Chang was nervously trying to glance at an old magazine, he caught his eye and winked.

"Well," said Hazzard in a loud voice. "It's just about time for the golden voice of the airways."

Kelly stopped playing cards and looked up. "Kate Smith sing-ing, 'When The Moon Comes Over The Mountain'. That was a long time ago . . ." He shook his head to snap himself out of his reverie and went over to turn on the radio.

The room suddenly became flooded with the singsong of Chi-nese music. "We shall now hear ten minutes of glorified, one-sided news," Kelly remarked as he went back to his cards and bottle.

The music stopped. A female voice made an announcement in Vietnamese, and after a short pause, the familiar voice of Hanoi Harry filled the room.

"This is Radio Hanoi, the voice of the people, with today's news in English. But first, a special message to our friends at Tu-Hao-Tuc. We would like to inform Mr. Michael Hazzard that we have completed all the arrangements, and have made a reservation for him at Apowan. He will be well taken care of when he arrives by ship tomorrow morning. And now, for today's news. The Soviet Union announced . . ."

There was a click as Chang turned off the radio. Maurice had stiffened and paused momentarily at Hanoi Harry's announcement, but now he was again monotonously throwing darts.

Kelly kept turning over cards without hesitation. "Well, what do you say now Mr. Michael Hazzard?" he said as he swept the cards together and shuffled.

"No more than I expected," replied Hazzard in a calm, even voice.

Maurice stopped his arm in midair and glanced over his shoulder.

Kelly slowly swiveled around in his chair and squinted at Hazzard.

Neither of them spoke. Hazzard grinned back and nodded sarcastically at their stupefied expressions.

"I expected them to find out about our plans—they always do," he reminded them. "So, I didn't plan on raiding the ammo dump at Apowan in the first place. The men and boats are all set to go somewhere anyway, and where we go doesn't make much difference as long as we bring back the ammunition."

Hazzard stood up and went to the bookcase where Kelly kept a supply of bottles and helped himself to a glass of raw whisky. Turning around, he found them still staring at him in disbelief.

"I'm going south, to Fhu-Dien. They'll be waiting for us up north." He raised his glass in a mock toast. "You see, just a matter of being smarter than the enemy."

Maurice shook his head and grabbed a steaming cup from a tray Wong had just brought into the room. The houseboy placed the remaining cups on the table next to Kelly.

"Well, now look at this," exclaimed Kelly, indicating the cups. "All kinds of strange things are happening tonight. We've got coffee instead of that damned tea for a change." He tasted the dark liquid and brought the cup down heavily on the table. "Agh! Tastes like cyanide. I'll stick to the locally made poison," and he gulped down a half glass of whisky. Wiping his mouth on the back of his hand, he looked at Hazzard. "Going to Fhu-Dien instead, eh?"

Maurice threw a dart at the poster. "So, you die at Fhu-Dien instead of Apowan." He threw another dart. "C'est la guerre!"

Kelly looked over at Chang with a twisted, sarcastic smile. "Turn the radio back on. I bet they find out about the switch before I finish this hand," and he went back to his game as though nothing had happened.

Chang looked across the room at Hazzard, who merely shrugged his shoulders and then belted down a big mouthful of whisky. There was nothing more to be done. From now, they could only wait and hope the spy would make a move.

Hazzard looked from Kelly to Maurice. Neither of them appeared to be upset over the change in plans. They had both been surprised when Hazzard had announced the switching of the raid from Apowan to Fhu-Dien, but this reaction would be normal for anyone. Now, they had accepted it, and fallen back into their usual monotonous pastimes.

Chang sat and began to watch the Frenchman throw darts. Kelly continued with his solitaire, pausing only to refill the glass he automatically drained each time he began a new hand.

Seating himself on the wide sill of a window facing the jungle, Hazzard began to amuse himself by blowing cigarette smoke through the coarse cotton netting at various inquisitive insects that were attracted by the light inside the room. He was becoming overly impatient, and found himself beginning to chain smoke. He looked at his watch. It seemed longer, but only ten minutes had gone by since Hanoi Harry had confirmed the fact the spy was still getting information out. Would the spy wait until morning? It did not seem probable. Hazzard was supposed to leave in twenty-four hours. If the spy waited much longer, it would become a difficult problem for the Reds to contact Fhu-Dien and set up an ambush in time to meet the raiding party. If anything was going to happen, it had to happen soon.

Hazzard glanced at Maurice and Kelly. Nothing had changed. Turning toward the window again, he was just about to blow a mouthful of smoke at a large, fat beetle when something passed swiftly across the rectangle of light that streamed from the window. Hazzard cupped his hands over his eyes and leaned into the netting. Someone was moving away from the building at an angle toward the jungle. Then Hazzard recognized the fleeting form. It was Wong, the houseboy.

Hazzard crushed his cigarette out on the window sill. How stupid can you be? he thought. He had overlooked one of the most obvious suspects. Wong, the ever present but silent houseboy.

Walking leisurely across the room, he bent down beside Chang.

"Stay here," he said in a low voice. "I'll be right back." Then, straightening up, he continued walking to the door, and out into the night.

Once outside, he ran toward the trees in the direction Wong had taken. Coming to the edge of the clearing, he found a small path leading away from the village. There was no alternative. Wong must have gone along the narrow trail. The undergrowth on both sides was too thick to walk through.

Pausing only for a moment to listen, Hazzard heard nothing but the night noises of the jungle. Then he started walking quickly and quietly along the path.

He had been along this trail once before, and remembered it ended abruptly at an old abandoned farmer's hut in the center of a small clearing about three hundred yards from the edge of the village. The moon was full and bright, and as he approached, he noticed how it gave the small hut a strange ghostly appearance outlined through the dark branches of the trees.

Again he stopped to listen. There was no sound except the constant drone of the myriads of insects—then came a flickering of light. Someone had lit a candle inside the hut, and the rays of light danced through the countless cracks in the tattered sides.

Hazzard reached inside his shirt and Sam appeared in his hand. Walking carefully across the open space that separated the hut from the jungle, he stopped beside the dried grass matting hanging down over the glassless window. Through a wide crack, he could see Wong assembling a portable military transmitter/receiver that was powered by a hand-wind generator. Working quickly, Wong soon had the earphones attached to the battery powered receiver crackling with static and odd bits of high-pitched Morse code. When Wong squatted down on the floor and began to compose a coded message, Hazzard knew that it was time to move.

Here was the one they had nicknamed George. Here was the one responsible for the countless deaths. Here was the one who had indirectly blinded Stürmer. These thoughts flooded through Hazzard's brain all at one time, like people trying to jam through Times Square on New Year's Eve, but one thought floated up above the rest. In one more minute Hazzard knew his assignment would be finished. All this, the hate, the eagerness, the overconfidence, was enough to blind his senses and the long years of former training, which should have alerted him to the fact there was another occupant in the hut.

Ramming his shoulder against the flimsy door, he charged into the small one-room hut, and was startled by the unexpected scream of a woman. The distraction was so sudden and unexpected that Hazzard momentarily forgot Wong and swung around to look into the wide-eyed face of a terrified young native girl.

The girl turned to run out into the night. Hazzard lunged to stop her, and Wong swung an age-hardened ax handle with all the strength he could muster.

The blow spun Hazzard sideways, and as he fell senseless to the floor, Sam exploded in a blinding flash as Hazzard's hand jerked spasmodically to involuntarily pull the trigger.

Wong kicked viciously at Hazzard's body, and then, realizing the immediate threat to his existence had been by-passed for the moment, he returned to the radio. He would deal with the stupid foreigner later.

The girl was gone. Now, he would have to turn the hand generator with one hand and send with the other. He finished coding the message and turned his attention to the receiver. Something was wrong. He turned the volume all the way up. There was no sound. Picking up the candle, be bent over for a closer look.

There was a neat, round hole on one side of the cabinet. On the opposite side was a large, jagged tear where the expanded 357 magnum slug had made its exit after smashing the wires and tubes.

He kicked savagely at the useless equipment. Then, glancing at the still form of Hazzard, Wong's lips curled back from his yellowed teeth as his mind spawned a clever plan.

In the corner of the hut was a five-gallon can of oil. Wong painstakingly spread it along the bottom of each wall. Setting the empty can by the radio, he walked to the door, stopping only long enough to spit vehemently at Hazzard's body.

Then, grinning with expectation, he held the candle to the dried grass sides of the hut. The oil would not explode like gasoline, and Wong knew he would be safely back in the village before the fire was discovered.

This would eliminate the bungling interference of the American, and allow him to escape to the safety of the communist troops encamped to the north.

From faraway in the distance, Hazzard seemed to hear the furious ringing of a temple gong, and the louder and closer sound of crackling wood. Consciousness came back with the sudden realization he was surrounded by fire. Opening his eyes, he saw one side of the hut was completely ablaze, and the flames were spreading across the ceiling.

The door was still untouched by the fire, and dragging himself up, he lurched through the light framework, to go rolling on the ground outside. Getting to his feet, he found Sam was still in his hand.

The hut was burning fiercely now, and the sound of the bell was pealing through the jungle as the guard on the cliff rang out the alarm.

Hazzard stood for a moment watching the fire and rubbing the side of his head as he tried to collect his thoughts. Then, remembering Wong, he jammed Sam into his waistband, and turned to run quickly toward the village. As he neared the clearing, groups of soldiers began to pass him on their way to the burning hut.

*   *   *

Wong had reached the village just as the alarm bell had begun to ring. As people and soldiers came pouring from their huts, he felt panic grip the muscles of his stomach. It was the age-old sensation of the cornered wild animal about to be caught. Not reasoning the confusion around him was due solely to the fire, and no one besides Hazzard knew of his traitorous activities, Wong, in his mind, suddenly became the hunted animal, and fear blinded his mind to everything except escape.

A group of soldiers was running toward him in the darkness, and he leaped quickly into the doorway of an empty hut. The soldiers passed, but Wong remained in his temporary haven of darkness. Then, the number of people running by the hut began increasing.

He looked back at the jungle as the flames shot high above the trees and illuminated the area with an eerie red glow. More people were passing, and as the flames rose higher, Wong recognized the form of Chang moving quickly along the path directly in front of him.

Chang shouted, and Wong turned to see Hazzard coming from the direction of the fire. Hazzard grabbed Chang by the arm and pulled him aside.

Wong watched as Hazzard talked and gestured toward the fire. His mind cleared, and his fear and panic were replaced by evil cunning as he realized even now, only Hazzard and Chang knew he was the spy. The confusion caused by the fire would make it impossible for them to organize a search for him. He dropped his hand to the hilt of the dagger at his waist. There was still time to complete one small item of unfinished business, then he could leisurely escape in one of the many motorized sampans tied up in the lagoon.

Again he was the quick-thinking intelligence agent he had always prided himself on being. He slipped out of the hut and faded into the shadows of the surrounding buildings. A wicked smile of self-satisfaction curled across his face—but he had failed to see the small form of Moro standing and listening in the darkness behind Chang and Hazzard.

*   *   *

Ling Ling Yung stood looking from the large window of the main room of the villa for a long time. The flames of the fire in the jungle had surged high above the trees and were now receding, but still no one came to tell her of the fire or its cause.

"Go and ask the reason of the fire," she commanded Ming Lee in Mandarin. When the giant Chinese had left, she turned again to the window, a furrow of worry creasing the smooth skin over her eyes. Without being told, she knew the flames had something to do with Hazzard. There are some things a woman does not have to be told, and icy fingers laced themselves around her heart.

The door opened behind her. "Put it on the table," she said in Mandarin, and Wong set the lacquered tray with its teapot and cups on a low carved table.

Ling Ling gave up her vigil at the window and seated herself as Wong poured the tea. Then, bowing low, he stepped away, and moved silently behind her chair.

Smiling constantly, he looked up and examined the room before him. He must make sure Ling Ling could not see him in the reflection of a window or a mirror. Satisfied his movements would not be seen, he reached inside his gown and brought out a long, slender dagger.

He had already decided his course of action. He would grab

Ling Ling by the hair and at the same instant plunge the blade sideways into her neck. From experience he knew this would prevent her from crying out, and he also knew death would be agonizingly slow.

Concentrating on the movements of Ling Ling's head, and overconfident with the murderous plan in his brain, Wong didn't hear the door behind him open softly. He raised the dagger, and his wrist was seized in a vise-like grip of steel. He froze as the cold sensation of panic flooded through the muscles and nerves of his stomach. Without looking, he knew he had bungled his way into the unyielding hands of Ming Lee.

There would be no reasoning with the blindly loyal giant. No excuses. No mercy. No pardon. Only death.

Ling Ling had leaped sideways when Ming Lee had grabbed Wong's wrist, and now she stood watching the silent battle. There was no fear in her eyes, only disgust for the cowardly attempt at assassination.

The pressure on Wong's wrist increased, and just before he thought the bone would snap, he released the dagger. The slow-witted Ming Lee, seeing the dagger fall to the floor, relaxed his grip, and Wong wrenched his arm free.

Springing to the sliding glass doors, Wong slammed them aside, and leaped over the railing of the veranda. Hitting the ground on all fours, he dashed headlong into the undergrowth that led toward the cliffs. There was no need to hesitate, for Wong had spent many hours here, eluding the guards so he could listen at the windows of the villa. There was but one thought in his mind now, the boats in the lagoon and escape.

Ming Lee went to the village as quickly as his large frame would permit. By now, the search was on. The fire had ceased to be of any importance, and Chang had organized a systematic search of all the buildings and surrounding area.

Ming Lee, unaware Wong was anything more than a deadly threat to Ling Ling Yung, grabbed everyone who came within his reach, picking them up and peering intently into their faces. Satisfied they were not Wong, he dropped the terrified individuals, and continued his search.

Hazzard had thought of the boats, and had stationed himself by the trail leading down to the lagoon. He had waited silently in the foliage beside the path for sometime when he heard the exhausted breathing of someone hurrying toward the cliffs.

Stepping from the bushes, he spun the dark figure around. It was the girl who had been in the abandoned hut with Wong. She struggled silently, trying to bite and scratch, but Hazzard held her arms pinned to her sides.

"Where is Wong?" he said in English, hoping the girl could understand. "Où ést Wong?" he asked in French.

At the sound of his voice, she stopped struggling and relaxed. Thinking the girl had now decided to stop fighting him, Hazzard released his grip on her arms, and found out immediately he had made a mistake. She took a quick step backwards. Suddenly he saw the flash of a steel blade, and felt the sharp edge against his forearm.

Hazzard made a lightening-fast grab at her small wrist and wrenched the dagger from her fingers before she could do any more damage.

Holding her tightly by the wrist, he was about to repeat the question when a short cry of terror echoed up from the darkness of the lagoon. It was followed by a long scream that could only come from a person in mortal pain. The sound of it made Hazzard's blood run cold, and the girl stiffened in wide-eyed fright.

Shoving the girl aside, Hazzard ran blindly down the sloping path toward the lagoon.

Coming to the stone wharf, Hazzard stopped. The figure of a man was rising slowly from a kneeling position at the far end. Hesitating for a moment, Hazzard shifted the girl's dagger to his left hand and drew Sam from his waistband. Then, he began to walk slowly and carefully toward the man.

There was no sound except the lapping of the water against the sides of the many boats, and as Hazzard drew nearer, the man turned to face him. It was Moro. He was holding a long, slender dagger, and both of his hands were covered with fresh blood. His shoulders hung limply, and his head was bent forward as he looked blankly at the ground.

His attitude puzzled Hazzard, and then, hearing a gasping moan, he looked beyond Moro and saw a man lying spread eagle at the edge of the wharf.

Pushing the unresisting Moro to one side, Hazzard looked down at the prostrate form. There, lying on his back, reaching with weak, shaking fingers toward his face and his bloody, empty eye sockets, was Wong.

Hazzard turned away from the grisly sight. He looked at Moro for a moment, then slowly trod his way back up the trail to spread the news that the spy had been caught, and already been tried and punished. Tried by Moro since the day Stürmer had returned with sightless eyes, and literally punished by the ancient law of "an eye for an eye".

*   *   *

19.
THE SACRIFICE

Hazzard lay on his bed, sleeplessly staring up at the folds of the mosquito netting above him. The excitement of the previous twelve hours had exhausted him beyond the point of sleep.

Wong had lived long enough to tell them the basic details of his nefarious activities. Doctor Kelly had tried to save the houseboy, but he had gone into shock after thirty minutes of questioning and within the hour he had died.

The Chinese telegraph book had been hidden in Kelly's office months before, when Wong had ceased to use it after memorizing a newer and simpler code. He had made it a practice to listen to all the conferences at the villa from outside the glass-paneled windows of the veranda. They were also surprised to discover Wong was fluent in French and had a good command of English, though he had pretended ignorance of anything that was not said in either Vietnamese or Chinese.

He had been sent to Tu-Hao-Tuc, disguised as a farmer among a group of refugees, by the commander of the Secret Police in North Viet Nam. He had forced the young native girl to work for him by threatening to have her father, who was still living in Hanoi, executed if she refused to obey him. Trained at the special intelligence school in Peking, he had been well chosen. Even Hazzard had to admit the houseboy had done his job with amazing efficiency and thoroughness.

Now, it was over. Hazzard knew he would soon be on his way back to Japan. He had received another note from Ling Ling Yung, and his thoughts ran to her as the first grayness of the coming dawn began to make the room grow brighter. She knew he would now be leaving, and she wished to thank him personally and say good-bye. He wondered if this last meeting with Ling Ling Yung would be as intriguing as the first.

Then, suddenly, the hand of fate reached out and changed the course of all the lives at Tu-Hao-Tuc. The furious ringing of the alarm bell began to echo across the village.

By the time Hazzard had dressed and found Chang, the distant sound of small arms fire could be heard coming from the north and west.

"What's going on?" asked Hazzard.

"The enemy troops that were encamped to the north are attacking," replied Chang. "We must evacuate the area as soon as possible. You can either help out at the lagoon and see that the refugees get aboard the boats, or you can take your men into the jungle. I can't order you to do anything—I can only ask."

Hazzard grinned. "I'll take my boys into the jungle. I'd never sleep nights again if I missed a chance like this. I've just got to know if that training I gave them did any good."

"Be careful. It will be very dangerous," advised Chang.

"Yeah, I already know that," grinned Hazzard as he turned to go in search of his men. "But for who—them or us?"

Hazzard found the men being issued ammunition at a large thatched roofed building that served as a warehouse. Runners were coming back at intervals from the jungle, and Hazzard soon pieced together the details of the attack.

The communist troops had split themselves into two forces;

one attacking from the north, the other from the west. They had run into Chang's patrols at dawn, and were slowly advancing toward the village. In about another hour they would come to the first line of prepared defense positions.

Hazzard decided to take his men to the north, as this area presented the enemy with the greatest possibility for a rapid advance.

Thirty minutes later, after double timing the men along the narrow paths and deploying them in the jungle, Hazzard heard the first sounds of mortar shells hitting the outskirts of the village. Instinctively, he knew the Reds would not just lob mortar shells around the area at random. They would have somebody stationed at a vantage point who could direct the fire for utmost effectiveness.

Sending two men with a pair of binoculars out onto a high promontory jutting out from the sheer cliff, he sent back for a rifle with a telescope sight.

Ten minutes later, the jungle in front of them erupted with the screaming cries of charging communist soldiers. Waiting until the Reds were less than thirty yards away, Hazzard gave the command to fire and was pleased at the results of the long sessions of rifle practice he had given the men. At the first volley, the charging Reds had faltered, and within seconds they had turned and fled back into the protection of the dense undergrowth.

As the firing died down, the man Hazzard had sent to the rear returned with an old Springfield rifle with a battered telescope sight crudely mounted on it. Hazzard could not trust the setting of the sight, and crawled out onto the overhanging cliff to zero it in by firing at stones along the rocky coast.

He finally managed to adjust the sight well enough to hit a ten inch object at three hundred yards. Then, he crawled up to the edge of the high promontory where the two men with the binoculars were excitedly beckoning to him.

Taking the glasses from them, he searched the area they pointed out, and soon caught the movement of a man among the branches of a tall tree. Small puffs of almost colorless smoke erupted from time to time from the jungle around the tree. These would be the positions of the mortars. Looking to the left, Hazzard found the man could get a clear view of the village from his vantage point above the jungle.

The range was almost four hundred yards from Hazzard to the tree, and rather than waste time zeroing in again for a longer distance, he decided to aim just above the distant figure and fired the rifle.

The first shot brought down a small branch to the left of the observer, but the man was too far away from Hazzard and the noise of the mortars too loud for him to notice he was being fired at.

Resting the Springfield firmly in a crack in the rocks, Hazzard took careful aim at a spot slightly above and to the right of the man's hunched up body. Slowly and carefully he squeezed the trigger until the recoil of the shot jarred the butt into his shoulder. Holding the rifle steady, he was rewarded with the sight of the observer falling through the branches to disappear into the thick foliage of the jungle.

Using a stick, Hazzard made pictures on the large flat rock to explain to the two men where to hold the cross hairs of the telescope sight in case the Reds decided to send up another observer. Leaving the Springfield with them, he crawled back along the rocks and into the jungle.

A quick survey showed him two of the men had been killed and one wounded. Since the first yelling charge, the Reds had stayed well hidden in the jungle and limited themselves to sporadic small arms fire that was not very effective, but the sound of bullets cutting through the leaves and branches was keeping Hazzard's men pinned to the ground.

Hazzard knew it was a hopeless and losing situation, and his only concern was to hold the communist troops off long enough for Chang to complete his evacuation of all noncombatants.

Abruptly, the enemy ceased fire, and Hazzard braced himself

for another screaming assault. The silence was suddenly punctuated by a loud pop, and looking up, he saw a red parachute flare drifting lazily over the tree tops. It was the signal to withdraw. Without being told, the men silently fell back. Half of them at first, then the remainder, each group stopping to cover the withdrawal of the other.

They had only covered a little more than a hundred yards when the Reds attacked. Finding no opposition, the communist soldiers grew bolder, and came crashing through the jungle at a fast run. Hazzard regrouped the men and they took up positions behind the larger trees and fallen logs. They let the communists come within point-blank range, and it was a slaughter. The Reds had become confused by the lack of fire and had bunched up as they ran forward. When the first shock of concentrated fire hit them, they milled around, bumping into each other, and ran about like blind men who had suddenly been caught in a burning building.

It seemed like an eternity, but the engagement lasted for only several minutes, then all was silent again. The ground before them was littered with the sprawled, dead bodies of the attackers. Hazzard's men paused only long enough to look at the scene in silent satisfaction, before continuing their orderly withdrawal.

When they came to the edge of the village, the Reds began to bombard the area again with mortar shells, and one remaining woman was running through the battle-torn streets hysterically screaming for her lost child. The men called to her but she paid them no heed. Then they saw the child, dirty and crying, waddling between the buildings. A mortar shell landed and splattered the area in front of the hospital with flying bits of mud. The woman screamed and ran toward the child.

The fluttering sound on an incoming mortar shell made the men throw themselves to the ground, yelling to the woman as they fell, but with only the thoughts of a mother for the safety of her child in her mind, the woman ran on.

Hazzard buried his head in his arms as the explosion shook

the area, and when he looked up again, the woman was lying face down in the middle of the street, her clothing ripped and torn from countless pieces of shrapnel. She had been between the explosion and the child, and in dying, had unknowingly protected her offspring by absorbing the lethal force that would have brought death to her baby.

The child, dazed by the explosion, now sat in the middle of the street, its face wet and dirty as it cried.

Two of the men rushed to the woman, turned her over, and left her as they ran to the child. Picking it up roughly, they continued to run toward the trail leading down to the lagoon. Hazzard knew without looking that the woman was dead, and he turned his head away. It was not good to have memories such as this to return and haunt you in your sleep.

Chang's troops were now running through the village in large groups, while here and there a few squads set up machine guns to hold off the advancing enemy.

There was no reason to stay longer in the village. Hazzard waved his men toward the boats, and then set off at a dogtrot along the trail to the top of the cliff above the lagoon.

He found Chang and Maurice looking at the village through binoculars, and seated on a rock among a small group of soldiers, was Stürmer, with Moro standing his perpetual guard behind him.

"The last of the refugees have been evacuated," Chang told him. "And in about ten more minutes all our troops will be out of the village. Everything is working very well."

Hazzard jerked his head in the direction of the German. "What's he doing here?"

"I don't know," replied Chang, and went back to watching the village through his binoculars.

Walking up to where Stürmer sat, Hazzard touched him on the shoulder. "Stürmer, you'd better go down and get in one of the boats."

"I shall wait for the last boat, Mr. Hazzard," came the calm, unemotional answer from the German.

"Look, Stürmer, this is no time for heroics," Hazzard said in a harsh voice, and reaching down, he grabbed Stürmer's arm. "Come on, get up," and Hazzard looked over at the impassive face of the little Oriental behind Stürmer. "Take him to the boats."

"No!" cried Stürmer angrily. "I will not be treated as an invalid. I will go when the others do—in the last boat!"

Hazzard had now lost his patience with the German and was about to jerk Stürmer to his feet when Moro laid a firm hand on his arm. There was something cold and deadly in the little Oriental's eyes that told Hazzard it was better to forget Stürmer and go about his business. Reluctantly he released the German's arm and went back to the large boulder where Chang was observing the village.

"It is almost time," Chang remarked. "The last of the men have pulled back from the village." He glanced back at Stürmer and lowered his voice. "What is wrong with Stürmer?"

"Nothing," Hazzard told him. "He's just being stubborn. He won't leave until the last."

Chang looked at Stürmer for a long time. "I wonder what we would do in his position?" he muttered half to himself.

Just then a group of soldiers carrying machine guns and wounded went by on their way to the boats, and one of them, turning to Chang, raised his rifle above his head with both hands.

"It means they are the last ones," explained Chang. "It is now time to give our guests a warm welcome." Turning to the small group of soldiers, he began to give orders in rapid Vietnamese.

The soldiers opened a large wooden box containing a complex array of storage batteries. Fastened to the inside of the cover was a large, two-pole knife switch. Uncoiling a large spool of wire, they attached the bare ends to the switch with thumb screws, and then stood back as though awaiting further orders. Chang inspected the box and the wires, and then sent all but two of them running down the trail to the boats.

"They are beginning to enter the village," said Maurice, who had been watching the movements of the enemy.

Chang looked at his wrist watch. "We will wait two more minutes."

Two minutes—one hundred and twenty seconds. A short space of time, but it can be an eternity when nerves are keyed up to the snapping point, and you must idly wait.

"Now, we shall teach them a lesson they will never forget," Chang said when the time was up. He squatted down beside the box, and everyone tensed.

Gritting his teeth, Chang closed the blades of the switch with a quick motion. Hazzard instinctively crouched down and bent his head. There was a long pause, and when the expected explosion did not come, Hazzard looked up to see a bewildered Chang open and shut the switch a second time.

The two soldiers rushed forward and examined the batteries and wires. There was a quick conversation in Vietnamese, then Chang stood up and turned to face the others.

"Something must have happened to the wires," he said wearily. "There is nothing we can do now. We must go down to the boats quickly. I will leave one man here for five minutes in case there are any stragglers." He looked down at the box of batteries. "We will leave the detonator like it is. There is still a slight chance it might go off."

Hazzard turned around to make sure Stürmer would be taken to the boats, but both the German and Moro were gone. Going to the edge of the cliff, he looked down the trail leading to the lagoon, but Stürmer was nowhere to be seen.

"Quick, come here," called Chang, and handing the binoculars to Hazzard, he pointed toward the village. "Along the trail to the village, just this side of the trees behind the hospital."

Hazzard put the glasses to his eyes, focused on the hospital and slowly swept the area. Stürmer, groping his way blindly from tree to tree, was heading for the village. Hazzard set the binoculars down on the rock. "The damn fool. He doesn't have a chance," and he started to run toward the village.

"Hazzard, stop!" cried Chang.

Hazzard turned around and saw Chang pointing a revolver at him.

"Come back here, Mr. Hazzard, and don't think I won't shoot you. If you make one more move in the direction of the village, I shall be forced to put a bullet in your leg."

"Are you crazy?" said the frustrated Hazzard. "He's blind. He's walking into a death trap!"

"Yes, I know," Chang replied grimly. "But if he were my own brother, I could not risk sending a man after him and waiting here. We have to leave now."

Anger and emotion drowned all reason from Hazzard's brain as he turned slowly and walked down the trail ahead of Chang to the last remaining boats in the lagoon. At the moment, he hated Chang, but later he would realize there was no alternative. The German, for some odd reason, had chosen to return to the village from which there was no escape, and the actions of one man could not be placed above the safety of the majority. It was the same in every battle that had ever been fought, but when it suddenly concerns a person closely associated with your life, a man was inclined to become emotional and forget the rules of war.

Hazzard jumped into a sampan and sat wearily in the bow, oblivious to the shouts of the soldiers as they poured gasoline on the boats that would be left behind, and turned them into floating infernos with lighted torches.

The man Chang had left on the cliff came running down the trail, leaped into the boat, and babbled to Maurice in French, between short, rasping gasps of breath.

"He is the last man," Maurice explained. "There is no one else."

No one but Stürmer, Hazzard thought bitterly, and he turned to look out at the sea as the soldiers began to scull the sampan through the lagoon.

*　　*　　*

Stürmer had overheard Chang's remark about the failure of the charges to detonate, and remembered seeing Wong crawling out from under the raised floor of the hospital one dark night. At the time, he had stepped into the shadows, and thinking nothing wrong, had let the houseboy pass unchallenged. He also recalled Wong had been carrying something in his hand. It was not until now that he realized it had been a pair of wire cutters. This, then, had to be the reason why the charges had failed to go off. The main wires from the battery detonator were buried alongside the trail leading to the village, and came up under the hospital. From there they radiated across the entire area. Cutting the main line under the hospital would prevent any of the buried charges from exploding.

Stürmer stumbled into the side of a building, and with searching hands, he felt the edges of the windows and ran his hands along the rough board siding. This was not the hospital, but the building next to it. Turning around, he placed his back against the wall, put one hand outstretched in front of his face, and walked slowly away from the building at what he hoped was a right angle.

Again, he misjudged. The next building was closer than he had anticipated. Though he had his hand up to protect himself, he slammed heavily into the wooden side. Working his way to the left, he reached up, and feeling the construction of a window, satisfied himself that this was the hospital.

There were twelve windows along the side, and the main line to the charges came out of the ground in the center of the building. Walking carefully and running his hands along the wall, the German began to count the windows. He had come to the fourth window when a communist soldier came around the corner of the building and stopped in surprise at the strange antics of the German. Then, slowly, the soldier brought his rifle up and took careful aim.

The sharp report of a rifle startled Stürmer by its nearness, and he froze against the wall, listening intently. No further sound came. Relaxing, he continued to feel his way along the side of the building.

Being blind, Stürmer had no indication Moro had followed him, and the small Oriental, not wishing to make his presence known, was very quiet as he withdrew his dagger from the side of the soldier whose reflexes had fired the rifle when the blade had penetrated his side. Wiping the dagger on the dead man's shirt, Moro picked up the rifle and silently followed Stürmer.

Coming to the sixth window, the German bent down and awkwardly crawled underneath the building. Moro could not understand what Stürmer was trying to do, but silently he followed, crawling underneath the building and taking up a position where he could not only observe the German's actions, but could protect him as well.

Crawling on his hands and knees, Stürmer began his grueling search for the wires. Turning on his side, he inched his way along, running one hand along the beams above him. Cobwebs, dust, and dirt fell from the rotting wood and gagged him. Sweat poured from his body and drenched his clothes. He had not realized how weak he had become, and every few minutes he was forced to stop and rest as he became dizzy with fatigue.

Finding no resistance, the communist troops were filtering into the village. When they suddenly realized the area was deserted, they began to enter the buildings, looting, breaking windows, and smashing furniture.

Stürmer had finally made his way to the center of the building and found the wires that came up from the ground alongside an upright. He knew there was a junction box fastened to the beams somewhere above him, and as his hand traced the wires, he found where one of them had been cut. Now, he had to find the other severed end, and being sightless complicated the task a thousand-fold.

Moro had been watching the progress of the German, and as Stürmer reached the wires and began to grope around with one hand, he realized what the German was searching for. Looking past Stürmer in the dim light, Moro could see the end of a wire coiled around another beam. Slowly, inching himself along on his elbows and knees, Moro wormed his way to the other end of the wire. Carefully he unwrapped it from the beam and moved toward Stürmer.

A hand grabbed the German's arm and he started in surprise. He reached out, felt the hand on his arm, worked his fingers up to the shoulder and over Moro's unresisting face.

"Moro!" he gasped, and the Oriental grunted.

Grabbing Stürmer's wrist, Moro pressed the end of the wire into the German's hand.

"Moro," Stürmer whispered slowly in French. "Go to the boats. Quick! I will give you time to get out of the village."

"Non!" said Moro, speaking in broken French. "We do this together."

Stürmer hesitated, and feeling the tense muscles of Moro's arm under his hand, he nodded his head and sighed. "Very well. We will do this together."

Each took a broken end of the wire and began to strip the insulation away from the heavy copper strands.

In the compound, the communist officers were directing the looting of the village. A large pile of objects was forming before them as the soldiers carried chests, pottery, furniture, clothing, and bottles from the buildings.

Groups of soldiers were tramping back and forth across the hospital floor above the heads of Stürmer and Moro as the Reds carried the remains of Doctor Kelly's supplies into the compound. Each time they heard footsteps, the German and Moro paused and waited until the soldiers left the building.

Finally, the ends of the wires were clean, and taking one in each hand, Stürmer waited. The sounds of soldiers moving about among the buildings were increasing, and he knew the Reds were coming in from the jungle in ever increasing numbers. A few minutes wait would make his and Moro's efforts all the more rewarding.

Stürmer's hands began to shake as he slowly brought them together. He needed courage more now than ever before in his life.

Pausing, he took a deep breath, and for some strange, unknown reason, he suddenly thought of the last passages from A Tale of Two Cities, it is a far, far better thing I do . . .

Then, suddenly, he laughed out loud at the ridiculousness of his wandering mind, and jammed his hands together.

The heavy charge of TNT buried beneath Stürmer and Moro went off simultaneously with the many other charges, sending clouds of smoke and debris high above the village, and a penetrating sound reverberating for miles through the jungle.

*   *   *

The deafening roar of the explosion fell heavily upon the long line of boats that stretched southward along the coast. Hazzard and the others watched silently as a great cloud of smoke and dust rose slowly over the cliffs and drifted inland. There were no words for times like these. Hazzard knew he had just witnessed a great act of sacrifice and heroism, and yet it was but a small and insignificant event in a world that seemed to be rushing headlong into self-destruction.

Hazzard lit a cigarette, leaned back against the gunwales of the sampan, and stared up at the small white clouds that pockmarked the sky. The events of the past few weeks would take a lot of forgetting—and he wondered how one went about forgetting images that had been indelibly burned into the mind.

*   *   *

20.

THE LAST PAYOFF?

" . . . *A*nd that, my little Oriental princess," concluded Hazzard as he sat with Michiko at the Champs Elysée in Akasaka Mitsuke, the only sidewalk café in Tokyo at the time, "is the story of Michael Hazzard, boy detective."

Michiko giggled, and Hazzard smiled. She was amused by the silly reference to himself, but Hazzard was reminiscing over the parts concerning Ling Ling Yung he had neglected to tell her. He still remembered the husky whisper of her voice in his ear as she said good-bye.

"We shall meet again," she had murmured, and her fragrance had come up to meet him as she pressed her body into his. For a fleeting moment her eyes had stared into his, trying to penetrate his innermost thoughts, and they seemed to say, "No matter where you are, or what you do, you are mine." At least Hazzard flattered his ego by making himself believe this was the unsaid meaning of that last look of Ling Ling Yung.

Then, it had been a long ride by junk along the coast and up the river to Saigon. A cargo plane to Manila, and a jet flight to

Tokyo. The next morning there had been a short telephone call to
Hazzard's office from Mr. Brown, in the best of Greenstreet voices.
Hazzard was to meet him at noon at the tables outside the Champs
Elysée café, and Brown would pay him the balance of the ten
thousand dollars.

"What time is it?" asked Hazzard.

"Almost twelve o'clock," sighed Michiko.

"Are you sure he said to meet him here?" he asked her.

Michiko looked at Hazzard and shook her head wearily back
and forth. "He said meet him at Champs Elysée sidewalk café, and
this is only sidewalk café in Tokyo, and it is called Champs Elysée.
Mike-san, this is third time you ask me same question in ten minutes."

Hazzard looked at his watch. "Well, it's twelve o'clock now.
Where is he?"

The voice of Greenstreet-Brown replied from directly behind
them. "I am right here, my dear Mr. Hazzard, and good afternoon
to you, Miss . . . ah . . ."

"Matsumoto," prompted Hazzard.

"Ah, yes. Mr. Hazzard's most capable, and I must say, extremely
pretty secretary." Brown wedged his large frame between the tables
and sat luxuriously on the chair beside Hazzard. The inevitable
briefcase was clutched across his lap, and he smilingly glanced
about, seemingly in the very best of spirits.

"My, but it is a fine day, isn't it?" he said to no one in
particular. "You know, other than the abominable rainy season, I do believe we have about the finest weather in the Orient, don't you?"

"Yes, I guess so," said the impatient Hazzard. "Now, Mr.
Brown, about our business arrangement . . ."

"Ah, yes, business," sighed Mr. Brown. "It is such a lovely day
I am inclined to forget business matters." Reaching into his briefcase, he produced three large, fat brown manila envelopes. "Which
will it be this time, Mr. Hazzard?"

"Japanese yen, if you don't mind."

"Here you are, Mr. Hazzard," and Brown handed two of the envelopes across the table. "The balance of your retainer. And it will not be necessary to sign a receipt."

"And not necessary to count it either," smiled Hazzard. "Well, now that it's over, we can relax and become friends. Would you care for a drink, Mr. Brown?"

"Not just at the moment, if you don't mind," and Mr. Brown dipped his hand once more into his briefcase. As he spoke again, he placed a small, flat wooden box on the table in front of Hazzard. "I have something here that . . ."

"Oh, no you don't. Not again!" exclaimed Hazzard, cutting Brown off in midsentence. "Come on, Michiko," and grabbing her by the arm with one hand and the manila envelopes with the other, he stood and dragged Michiko quickly through the tables. They ran to the edge of the street, flagged a passing taxi, and zoomed off in the best of kamikaze styles.

Mr. Brown, as outwardly unperturbed as an English gentleman lounging on the veranda of the Raffles Hotel in Singapore, sighed and calmly lifted Hazzard's untouched, and now warm cocktail from the table. After an exploratory sniff, he relished a small mouthful, replaced the glass on the table and sighed again.

A very slick-looking, dark-skinned Oriental slid noiselessly into Hazzard's vacant chair, and folded his hands on the table. His white sharkskin suit, dark tie and Panama hat, though strikingly clean and well pressed, seemed out of place with the background of modern Tokyo.

"What was his answer?" asked the man in the sharkskin suit.

"I really don't know," said Brown as he tasted the warm cocktail for the second time. "I didn't even get the chance to ask him." His eyes fell on the unopened wooden box. "And I shall have to visit his office shortly. Ling Ling Yung would never forgive me if I failed to deliver her small gift to Mr. Hazzard."

He set the empty cocktail glass on the table, placed the small wooden box and the remaining large, fat brown manila envelope back into his briefcase and sighed.

"I shall ask him in a few days. I have no doubt he would enjoy working with us."

Then, he turned his head and beckoned to the waiter. "Bring me another one of these, whatever it is you call them, and one for Mr. Wu, here. Oh, and yes, do not use any ice. They are excellent when they are warm."

*   *   *

Printed in the United States
947300002B

9 781401 060695